BOOGER MCCLAIN OZARKS DETECTIVE SERIES BOOK 7

MIRROR
IN THE
SHADOWS

ALAN
BROWN

BRIAN
BROWN

World Castle Publishing, LLC
Pensacola, Florida
Copyright © 2024 Alan Brown & Brian Brown
Paperback ISBN: 9798891262997
eBook ISBN: 9798891263000
First Edition World Castle Publishing, LLC, November 11, 2024
http://www.worldcastlepublishing.com
Licensing Notes
Cover: Karen Fuller
Editor: Karen Fuller

CHAPTER 1
THE LUCKY DAY

Don't ever assume tomorrow
While the clock still runs on today
For all around you is peril,
Desperados, violence, decay.
We can see the dawn brings morning,
And the daylight sings its song,
But the moon reflects – a mirror, my friend
And the night's shadows are long.

The stalker wasn't like other men. Any close observer could tell. As it was, however, no one was watching him when he pulled his dealer-plated blue Honda Civic hatchback into the Battlefield Mall parking lot and slowly drove down each aisle. He was an invisible observer, and there was much to see. So many cars, so many young women shopping.

The stalker parked in a space with a direct view of the main entrance. There, he watched and waited for his prey. He thought of himself as a hunter in a tree stand, looking for the perfect buck. Two hours went by. He had seen many attractive women. Some young, some older, some by themselves, and some with children or husbands or girlfriends. However, none had sparked his interest.

Then, a silver Lexus SUV pulled into the lot several rows away. He watched and waited for the driver to exit. When she did, he sat up in his seat. "She's the one," he said to himself. The Lexus lady was tall, with long, flowing blond hair. She wore a red sundress, which was short enough to show off her lanky, tanned legs. His time patiently waiting had paid off. "She's perfect," he thought.

The stalker was tempted to follow her in the mall, but he worried he could lose her. It was busy. She'd be back for her car eventually, and he knew he could be patient a while longer. While he waited, he moved his car to be closer to hers. He got out and pretended to head to the entrance before turning around just so he could walk slowly past her car. It was a newer model, clean. No booster seats or obvious signs of children.

Two hours went by before the lady returned to her car. It was nearly 4 pm. "If she had kids, they were likely home from school by now. If she had a husband, he would be coming home from work soon." So many things could ruin his plans. He would make his decision when she arrived home.

The Lexus pulled out of its parking space and headed toward the mall exit. The unassuming stalker, fitted in a plain brown hat and large dark sunglasses, followed far enough behind her so as not to get noticed. Being undetectable was the key to his thrill. He couldn't be spotted. If he was, the game was over.

She turned right out of the parking lot and drove north to Sunshine Street. She went about a mile and made another right into a subdivision of well-kept, upper-middle-class homes. A left and then another right. The stalker was careful to stay back. His heart was racing. She waved to a neighbor. He slumped back in his driver's seat, hiding behind tinted windows. Soon, his target pulled into a driveway, and the garage door began to open. This was the moment of truth. If there was another car in the garage, if there were any bicycles or toys or other signs of children being present, or if she closed the garage door, the stalker would make a note of the address and leave. The lady would still become a victim, just not that day.

He was careful. He never attacked someone unless the opportunity was exactly right. Once, he waited nearly a year. Everything had to be just so. It was part of the thrill.

But, on this day, there were no other cars in the garage. There were no bicycles, swing sets, or toys in the yard. On this day, the lady chose to leave her garage open while she got things out of her trunk.

The salesman parked his car adjacent to a small park just across from the subdivision. He got a black bag full of useful goodies from his trunk and walked nearly two blocks back to his victim's house. The garage was still open. He noted that items still remained in the trunk. He couldn't believe his luck.

He approached the house slowly – looking for as long as he could as someone who was going anywhere else in the neighborhood. He liked to imagine that if a nearby homeowner was watching him, he'd look like a guy who belonged. Like a guy who had borrowed a bag of gardening supplies from another neighbor and was returning them. His gate was casual as he turned to walk up his target's driveway. She had made one last trip to the trunk and grabbed two bags. Her back was to him.

She was more beautiful than he thought. A large diamond wedding ring caught his eye. She was married. Her husband would be home soon. He glanced at his watch: 4:30 pm. That didn't leave him much time.

The two bags were the last in her trunk. She closed the hatch and walked to the door inside the garage. With the stalker now just feet away from the back of her car, she pushed the automatic garage door closer on her way into the house. As the door shut, he ducked below and moved inside quickly, quietly. Her hands were full, and she didn't lock the door behind her. It was the final break he needed. He could have been trapped inside the garage and needed to press the automatic opener to get out. He had been bold, and it paid off. The door to the house was unlocked, and he walked straight into the mudroom. From there, he could see the target in the kitchen. He quietly moved closer. When her back was turned, he made his move – setting his bag down on the counter and grabbing her around the neck and mouth all in one swift motion. He placed a piece of duct tape over her mouth so she couldn't scream and dragged her into the bedroom while she was kicking and thrashing about, trying to get free. The stalker threw her on the bed and tied her hands to the headboard of the bed and her feet to the bed posts. She was utterly incapacitated.

The next were terrifying moments for Sally. Her name was Sally Rogers. She was from Kansas City. She loved puppies and babies, crime novels, and peppermint mochas. She had been in love three times. He sexually abused her. She fought, tried to negotiate through the duct tape, and then relented. She hoped she could stall him somehow so her husband would arrive to save her.

When the stalker was done, he placed his black bag on the bed, opened it, and pulled out a phone wire. He wrapped it around Sally's neck and strangled her. Her last moments of life were spent in prayer. She prayed for her family. When all motion left her body, he placed his gloves and phone cord back in the bag and left the house through the front door, leaving it unlocked.

It was her husband who found his wife when he arrived home from work at nearly 6 pm. The police arrived at the house a short time later. They would find the front door unlocked and assume that was the way the murderer got inside the house. There would be no clues except for the semen, and it would be weeks before they determined if there was a hit after running that clue through their national database.

The alarm went off at 5:30 am. Rose woke, brushed her teeth, got dressed, and went into the kitchen. It was Thursday. She always made cinnamon rolls for Booger on Thursdays. This day was no exception. She got out the wheat flour and other ingredients and made six large rolls. Two were for Booger, one for her, and four for any clients that happened to stop by. Lately, there hadn't been many.

While the rolls were still warm, she wrapped them in a cloth and headed toward the office. The office was in the same building as their home. The home was on the ground floor, and the office was on the third floor. On the way, she stopped outside the front door to pick up the morning paper.

Once in the office, she turned on the lights and made a pot of triple-strength Folger's coffee. It would be needed to wake Booger up enough to be civil. He was a bear in the morning before his first cup.

Then, she put the paper down on Booger's desk. He always read the paper and drank his coffee before getting down to work. Lately, new jobs had been slow but there were plenty of unsolved cases for him to work on. After reading the newspaper, drinking his coffee, and eating his cinnamon roll, Booger would go to his war room. That's what he called it, anyway. It was the place where he kept all the old case files. It was also the place where he kept all his notes on new cases he was working on.

At 6:10 am, the private investigator walked into the office. He didn't say a word to his wife. She didn't say a word to him. That was normal. It was an unspoken rule between them to not talk about anything until he'd had some coffee. He went to his desk, sat down in his recliner, and began to read the newspaper while he sipped on his strong cup of Joe. Rose shut the office door to give her husband some privacy. Booger used that opportunity to open his desk drawer and pull out a pint of fine rye whiskey. He poured two fingers of whiskey into his cup and took a long, slow sip. "Ahh, that tastes good," he said under his breath.

Rose knew about the whiskey in Booger's drawer. She didn't approve, but she never said anything. She believed in choosing her battles, and a little booze in his coffee was something she could let slide.

After about 15 minutes, Rose entered Booger's office.

"Want a refill?" she asked.

"Yes, sweetie. Thanks."

"Anything interesting in the paper?"

"Yes, a young woman was murdered in her home yesterday."

"Oh, that's terrible. Do the police know who did it?

"A psychopath," Booger said to his wife.

"Why do you say that?"

"It appears he followed her home from the mall. That's where the paper said she had been last. He must've found her there."

"But why the mall?" Rose replied.

"Numbers," Booger replied. "It was the place where the largest number of women were gathered in one place. He was looking for a specific type, I imagine. He probably had a clear view of the entrance."

"Why didn't he go in the mall? Inside, he would have likely found his victim sooner."

"Yeah, but he would have taken the risk of being seen. Besides, the crime was never going to take place at the mall. He intended it to happen at the victim's house or apartment. He needed to remain in his car, ready to follow the victim to wherever she was going."

"So how, or umm, why did he pick her?"

"I'm not sure. She would have been a certain type, a certain look. The paper says the victim was blonde, blue eyed, and with a thin build. Maybe he was looking for blondes; maybe it was the dress that caught his eye."

"She was married, right?"

"Yes."

"Maybe he was a hired killer? Maybe the husband hired someone to do away with her."

"Possible, but doubtful. A husband who hired a hitman would want a quick death. He wouldn't want his spouse to suffer. Besides they were almost newlyweds, married less than a year. All indications were that they had a happy marriage. Plus, there was a car."

"A car?"

"Yes, a blue sedan of some kind. The newspaper says a neighbor spotted the car driving slowing down the street but was unsure about the model – either that or the police are holding back that detail. Anyway, the neighbor waved to the lady who got murdered as her car went by and then noticed the suspect's vehicle a few seconds later. Police are said to be checking security cameras at the mall for more information about the suspect."

"So, who was the victim?"

"Sally Rogers, the paper says. She was married to Henry Rogers less than 11 months ago. They just recently moved into the house on James Street."

"From all accounts, the marriage was good. Henry said they were planning to have a family. That he and his wife were soul mates and loved each other very much."

"Yeah, well, what do you expect him to say? The husband is always the first person the police investigate when the wife gets murdered."

"He had a solid alibi, Rose. He was at work. There were several co-workers who could back him up. No, I don't think the husband did it. Everything points to the man in the blue car."

"Why do you think he did it?"

"He's a psychopath. No use in asking why. He didn't see her as a real person. Just an object. A thing to control for a time. That's how these wackos think."

"Do you think he'll strike again?"

"Absolutely, unless the police catch him first. It's just a matter of time. His mind has gone to the dark side, so to speak, so nothing will satisfy him but blood lust. He might be careful for a while. Lay low and all. But he won't stop. And there is nothing short of being captured that will stop him."

Booger put the newspaper down and took a sip of coffee. It was cold now, and Booger's expression when he took a sip showed his disapproval.

"Let me get you a fresh cup," Rose said.

"Thanks, sweetie. Can you get me one of your cinnamon rolls too?"

"Booger, you know what the doctor said about your high cholesterol."

"It's just one more cinnamon roll, Rose. And we

shouldn't waste them. They are so good."

"Well, I guess if you're careful with lunch, it would be fine."

"Right. Of course," he said, with no real intention of being careful for lunch. Booger didn't really trust doctors. They might know what's best for people generally, he thought, but they didn't know what was best for him.

Booger and Rose had been married for nearly two years, marrying late in life. They had known each other for nearly 40 years and were friends long before they tied the knot. Rose knew Booger as well as she knew herself. She knew her husband was going to do exactly what he wanted to do regardless of the consequences. Damn the high cholesterol. Booger would eat what he wanted to, but not in front of Rose. His love for her was too strong to disappoint her. When she was around, Rose was the boss. What she told him to do, he did. What she served him to eat, he ate. Even the cinnamon rolls she made were doctored to be healthier for her husband with whole wheat flour and a sugar substitute. He learned to adapt, but he would cheat on his diet anytime he had the chance.

Booger put his paper down and sat up in his recliner as Rose entered his office carrying a hot cup of Folgers and a plate containing one of her freshly baked cinnamon rolls. She sat it down in front of her husband, then walked behind the desk and gave Booger a gentle kiss on the cheek.

"Are you done with the paper now, hun?"

"Yeah, I'm done."

Rose picked it up and walked out of the office. Every morning was the same routine. Rose would take the paper after Booger finished it, close his office door and she would go into the reception room, sit at her desk, and work the crossword puzzle in the paper while sipping her own cup of coffee.

They were creatures of routine, completely comfortable with doing things exactly the way they had been doing them ever since they got married. Rose would wake up first. She would bake her Danishes or cinnamon rolls or blueberry muffins and take them up to the office on the third floor. On the way, she would stop at the front door and pick up the morning paper. Once in the office, she would put the newspaper on her husband's desk and then make an extra strong pot of Folger's coffee. By then, it would be nearly 6 am, which was the time Booger woke up. Every day was the same. It was comfortable. There was safety in the routine.

That day had been no different than the others, except she could tell Booger was fixated on the murdered woman.

Rose knew her husband well enough to know that this case was one that Booger intended to get involved in, somehow, someway.

"Do you think this was his first victim?" she asked her husband.

"No. It might have been his first in Springfield."

"What makes you think that?"

"Everything was done well as if he had done this at least a few times before. A psychopath gets better at what he does the more crimes he commits. Judging from the lack of clues, I would assume this guy knows what he's doing. And a hunter can't use the same hunting grounds for long. He may have just moved to Springfield."

"Hmm. And you're certain he'll strike again?"

"Absolutely."

"You're going to try to find him, aren't you?"

He paused for a moment. "Absolutely."

CHAPTER 2
THE JOGGER

The morning spoke to him like a whisper. It's time to go. Ben Sawyers put his running shoes on, strapped a backpack over his shoulders, and headed out the front door of his home in north Springfield. He often jogged before dawn since his wife left him. He didn't sleep much anymore, and running gave him energy for the day. It got him moving. This morning, however, he had a different purpose for jogging.

Running used to be so easy for him. That was before he married Mary. That's when he gave up jogging so he wouldn't wake her up. He gave up a lot of things for her. Ten years of not running, coupled with gaining twenty pounds, slowed him down considerably, and it was more challenging than before. He had neither the endurance nor speed he used to have. Still, jogging was a passion, and he was determined to do it even if he was slower these days.

Ben Sawyers was forty-six with a thin build, short, wiry brown hair, and balding on top. He had been told he was handsome for his age, but he was not a ladies' man. He was quiet, shy, and liked to keep to himself. Ben was a loner who changed jobs frequently. He had gone through twelve jobs in the last ten years. "That was one reason Mary left me," he said to a neighbor recently. "She got tired of me not having a steady job." It wasn't true. He killed her.

As he jogged the streets of Springfield, his mind went to a time when he was still a teenager and living in a small two-bedroom ranch-style house in Wichita. That night, his father was drunk. More drunk than normal. His dad had lost his job earlier that day and had turned to the bottle to cope with his depression. The drinking started in the late afternoon at Shockers' Tavern, which was just a couple of blocks from home.

He downed a half dozen shots of bourbon with beer chasers – one shot for each can. By the time Ronald got home at 9 pm, he could barely walk. Ben's dad was a nasty drunk. He beat his wife Janie on numerous occasions, and that night was no exception. At first, Ben stayed in his room as his dad picked a fight with his mother, just like any other night. But he wouldn't stay there long. This night was different. His mother's beating was more severe and lasted longer than any time before. His mother's screams echoed in his ear. He was afraid his father was going to kill her. Ben decided to help his mom, even though he was sure that would mean he'd get beat. He ran to the master bedroom and tried to pull his dad off his mother. That's when his father turned his rage on his son. A punch in the stomach took the boy's breath away. A punch to the face sent Ben backwards and onto the floor.

Ben, with his father staggering toward him, jumped to his feet and ran. He ran to the living room and into the kitchen. His father was not far behind. The only escape from the kitchen was the basement, so Ben opened the door and raced downstairs. When he turned around, he saw his father at the edge of the stairs. His mother was directly behind the father. Then he saw his dad fall, rolling headfirst down the full flight. When he landed at the bottom of the stairs, his father's neck was broken.

When the police arrived, both Ben and his mother gave the same story. Ronald was drunk and chased his son down the steps to the basement and fell on his way down. But Ben knew the truth, and it was something he would have to live with from then on. It was something he couldn't help but think of from time to time. Ben wished he would have been stronger. He wished he could've fought him properly. He never blamed his mother. His mother saved him.

It was that something on his mind at 4 am as he headed out into the dark, cool morning.

"Damn, I love this time of day," he said to himself, as he adjusted his backpack. It was as if he was invisible to the world. The darkness was the perfect cover. As people slept in their homes, he ran past them. He loved knowing they were completely unaware of the danger just outside their windows.

There was plenty of time to think on this lonely run and Ben's mind focused on his failed marriage. He had met Mary almost twelve years earlier on a Christian dating site. She was Catholic. He was just trying to find himself a born-again Christian. He hoped God could give him the answers he was looking for. He prayed that the Almighty could cast out the demons that had taken over his life. If God could just soften the urges in his heart, he thought he could have a normal life. That's all he wanted.

For months, they wrote back and forth, getting to know each other. Finally, Mary suggested a meeting. She lived nearly two hours away on a farm ten miles south of Clinton. She agreed to come to Springfield so they could have dinner together.

They met at the Red Lobster on South Glenstone that Saturday night. Ben bought a new suit for the occasion. He was nervous. More nervous than he could ever remember. He felt like he was auditioning for a new life, playing the role of a decent person. Would he be believable, he wondered? They had never even seen pictures of each other. Ben had no idea what Mary looked like.

"I'll be wearing a red dress," Mary told him.

On the evening of their first meeting, Ben showed up at the restaurant thirty minutes early. He sat in the lobby and waited for her to arrive. Five minutes before their agreed meeting time, a heavy-set woman in her early twenties walked in alone wearing a red dress.

Ben stood up as she approached. "Are you Mary?" he asked.

"Yes, and you must be Wade for me," she replied.

"Excuse me," he said. He could have sworn she said, "Wade."

"Ben Sawyers. You must've been waiting for me."

He couldn't help but laugh. "Ha! Yes, of course."

Ben Sawyers had a sordid history. His name was legally changed to Wade Collins years before he met Mary. When he moved to Springfield from Wichita, he knew it was time to ditch the name. Ben was his birth name, and Sawyers was like the last name he had as a child growing up in Eastern Missouri: Squires. Wade Collins was a dirty name. It was tainted to him. He didn't want to be that person anymore. As it turns out, Mary will never learn that he had ever been anything but Ben Sawyers.

The dinner that evening was unremarkable. Neither could recall what they had to eat a year later. But the conversation and the chemistry between the two of them was notable. Ben had only been on two dates before. He was awkward, shy, and quiet during those two dates. But not that night with Mary. She had the gift of gab and dominated most of the conversation, and he was glad for it. They worked well together. She talked, and he listened. Mary talked about church and God, about her family, and about life in a small town. He felt comfortable. A church-going woman who could let him be quiet. She was perfect.

The two were inseparable after that first date. They would marry less than a year later in a small chapel in Clinton. Mary wanted Ben to move to the farm and learn the family business, so he gave up his job in Springfield. He was more than happy to take on her life and her family's identity. Mary's father, Allan, was in his sixties and had health problems. His wife, Mary's mother, was domineering like Mary.

The hope was that Ben would learn the family business and take it over from Allan when he was ready to retire. In the beginning, that plan seemed to be working.

Ben settled into farm life quickly. This was the opportunity that he had been searching for. He genuinely wanted to start fresh, to be good, or what he thought was good. He mostly enjoyed church on Sundays, and he didn't hate working on the farm the other six days of the week. It was hard, but it gave his life structure. He had purpose. He was disciplined. For a time, anyway.

Mary was kind and gentle and understanding with him at first, and so was her father. But after the newness of the situation wore off, things changed.

Mary was headstrong from the beginning and was raised in a black-and-white world. Her father spoiled her, and constantly talked of things being either good or bad. People were either helpful or obstacles to be overcome. Their family knew friends and enemies but no one in between. Allan raised Mary to be strong and independent, but as he often noted, those things came naturally. One of the first stories Allan shared with Ben about Mary was the time in fourth grade when his daughter beat up little Joey Buccholz for cutting in the lunch line.

"Mary was suspended for a week, and I bought her ice cream every day," Allan said with a laugh. "I'm not raising no sissy girl. I told her she needed to stand up for herself. She had to be tough because the world was tougher."

Not surprisingly, Mary was a demanding wife, and

Allan became a critical boss and father-in-law. Nearly everything Ben did was met with criticism.

"You're lazy. You're useless," Mary told him more times than he could count. "I don't know why I married you."

The verbal attacks on him were part of daily life. Ben, however, never talked back. Where he was from, he couldn't talk back without getting hit in the mouth. Much like with his father, Ben was completely submissive until the one time he couldn't take it anymore.

Allan had been drinking most of that day. He had always been a heavy beer drinker, but that day was much worse. He had settled down in his leather recliner, watching a ballgame with a six-pack of Budweiser iced up next to him on the coffee table. Mary was on the sofa next to him, barking orders at her husband. Allan turned his attention on Ben when he accidentally knocked over one of his father-in-law's beers. "What the hell is wrong with you?" he yelled. "You're a no-good son of a bitch! I have no idea why my daughter married you."

The demeaning remarks went on from there. Each one ratcheted up the pressure inside his head. Ben didn't say a word until he finally exploded. He got in Allan's face when he was being berated.

"What are you going to do, you little punk? You don't have the nerve to do any..."

But before Allan could finish his sentence, Ben grabbed his father-in-law by the face and flung him across the room and into the wall. Allan was knocked out instantly, and Mary screamed in shock and horror.

Ben ran after him, hitting Allan twice as he was slumped over near the coffee table.

That's when Mary first saw Ben's dark side. He nearly killed her father that night. Mary had to drag her husband out of the house as he screamed at her unconscious dad, "That's what I'm going to do!"

Ben was no longer welcomed on the farm. Half terrified and half impressed, Mary dipped into her father-supported savings and moved with her husband to Springfield two days later while Ben looked for a job.

For a time, Mary changed. She was nicer and more attentive. He had, after all, stood up for himself, which earned her respect. So, for a few months, married life was pleasant for them both.

But the old Mary slowly reappeared. She was tired of Springfield, and in her mind, Ben couldn't do anything right. He didn't earn enough money. Their house wasn't nice enough. Ben wasn't attentive enough to her in her mind. She soon resented him.

Mary didn't work. She never attempted to find a job. In her mind, a woman's place was in the home. Ben couldn't keep a job. He'd work for a month or two and get fired, usually for losing his temper over something small at work. He was always on edge. Her husband was constantly going from one job to another, most paying little money. They lived in a small, 2-bedroom house south of Kearney in the older, north side of Springfield.

In fairness, Mary had reasons to be upset with Ben, but she certainly wasn't making the situation better by refusing to find a job and constantly harassing her husband. Their marriage was at a breaking point, but it wasn't her treatment of him that finally caused their marriage – and her life – to come to an end.

That was Murphy's doing. Murphy was a six-year-old, part lab, part retriever – a stray Ben picked up one stormy night two blocks from home. The dog was wandering the streets searching for food. He brought her home to Mary's objections. She fought with Ben for two days about keeping the dog until he finally assured her that she wouldn't have to take care of Murphy. He would do everything, and the dog would stay in the small work shed that Ben had in the backyard.

"You won't see or hear Murphy. I'll feed and walk her and clean up her messes. She'll stay in the shed behind the house," he told his wife.

That seemed to work for a short while. But Ben began spending more and more time in his shed or on long walks with Murphy. Before long, Mary became obsessed with the dog and regularly ridiculed her husband any time she happened to see her or she was mentioned.

"I know. Instead of getting and keeping a real job, why don't you spend more time with your stupid mutt!" she said one day. "You're lucky I don't euthanize it."

His only peace and quiet came during the time he spent with Murphy. The dog didn't judge him, didn't argue with him, and certainly didn't belittle him. Murphy became his respite from his hellish marriage.

That all changed once Ben was involved in a life-threatening accident. He was driving home from his job at Hardee's one cold, icy night in February when his car slid on a patch of black ice and ran head-on into a large truck on Highway 65. The fire department had to pry him out of the car. An ambulance took him to Mercy Hospital, where he would stay for seven days. He had two broken ribs, a punctured lung, and a severe concussion. When he finally returned home from the hospital, the first place he went when he got home was the storage shed.

"Murphy, I'm home," he yelled when he opened the shed door. But Murphy didn't run and greet him like she had done every time before. Murphy wasn't in the shed.

He rushed back to the house to ask his wife where Murphy was.

"She's gone. I took her to the dog pound because you weren't home to take care of her."

"How long ago?"

"I don't know, five or six days, I guess."

It was then that you could see the rage in Ben's eyes. The bad Ben was back.

At first, he said nothing. He grabbed a shovel and started digging in the backyard as he let his feelings build to a boil while he planned his next steps.

"What are you doing out there in the rain?" Mary asked, annoyed.

He looked up at her slowly. "Every dog needs a grave."

"Your stupid dog isn't here! Are you dumb?"

That night Ben stayed up when his wife went to bed. In the early morning hours, when Mary was sound asleep, he went to his shed. Inside it, he grabbed a hammer. Then he went back into the house and walked straight to the bedroom where Mary slept. One strong swing of that hammer would have done the trick, but Ben's rage took over, and twelve swings of the hammer later, there was little left of his wife's head.

He buried her in that backyard grave. The next day, he would plant a tree directly above Mary's gravesite. It was a beautiful Cherry Blossom tree, Mary's favorite.

It took Ben nearly a week to clean up the crime scene and get rid of his wife's things. He'd eventually wipe down her phone and throw it out his car window and into a ditch north of Bolivar so it would seem as if she was on her way to the family farm. About eight weeks after that violent night, Allan came to Springfield looking for her.

"I've been trying to call her for weeks. She never goes this long without talking to me," he said from Ben's front porch, standing in the rain. "I know something is wrong, and I know you're to blame."

"She left me two months ago while I was in the hospital. All I came home to was a note. She said she was moving back with you. Her things were gone. She's your problem now," Ben said before slamming the door in his father-in-law's face.

Two days later, a police officer came to his house. Ben gave a statement.

"I was recovering from my accident. When I finally came home, she was just gone," he told the officer plainly. "No, I didn't hold onto the note. There was nothing sentimental about it. Ours wasn't a good marriage. I couldn't keep a job, and she didn't want to work. I didn't expect her to leave, but I wasn't surprised either."

That was the last he heard from anyone connected to his wife. And from then on, Ben was wild. He did exactly what he wanted to do.

Five miles into his run, Ben turned into Southern Hills – an upper-middle-class subdivision south of Sunshine with a bunch of mid-century homes. The streets were winding, the houses were spacious, and the lawns were well-manicured. It was a part of town Ben had always wanted to live in.

Once he entered Southern Hills, he slowed his jog to a walk. He was tired from his run, and he wanted to save some strength. As he went, he noted the addresses on each mailbox. After about ten minutes or so of walking, he stopped. "This is it." There, he took his backpack off and opened it. Inside was a mask, gloves, rope, knife, and a thin metal tool for popping locks. "Only one car in the driveway. I should be good," he thought.

He took everything but the rope out of the bag and put the mask and gloves on. Then he went to the back of the house to a sliding glass door fronting the walk-out basement. It was locked, but a few movements of the metal tool between the lock and the door were enough to open it.

From there, he walked up two flights of stairs to a floor that had four bedrooms and two baths. The first bedroom contained a home office. The second and third bedrooms were occupied by two young children. "What? Oh, no." The fourth bedroom was the master suite. Inside were a young husband and wife sleeping in the bed. This wasn't part of the plan. He'd understood the husband and kids were supposed to be visiting his mother's house at Lake of the Ozarks.

Ben had spotted his prey a week earlier at Price Cutter. He'd overheard her flirting with a man behind the deli counter, indicating they could get together when her husband went out of town. She was young and attractive with short blond hair and a red-striped dress. "It's fate," he thought. He watched as she loaded the groceries in the trunk of her car and then followed her into Southern Hills in a gray dealer-plated Toyota Corolla. He stayed back but saw her pull into her spacious mid-century home and made a mental note.

This wasn't how he wanted to do things. He had a soft spot for kids. He saved his anger and hatred for adults. Kids were usually victims, and he didn't like knowing he was creating victims. "It's one thing if they come home and mommy's gone..." He had to make a quick decision. He could leave the way he came and pray he hadn't woken anyone up, or he could proceed. "I'm too far in to back out now."

He used the knife to bludgeon the husband first. He cut his neck and vocal cords in one fast slash. The husband was sound asleep when the knife first penetrated his body, so it made minimal noise. It did, however, wake his wife, who began to scream. Ben rushed to cover her mouth while he was covered her husband's blood. Finally, the husband stopped moving so he could concentrate his attention on his wife. He promised her he would let her live if she kept quiet and didn't wake the children. He promised her that he would be gentle and not hurt her. His promises turned out to be lies.

After the attack, Ben cleaned the bloody knife in the sink in the master bath, put it away in his backpack along with his mask and gloves, changed his shirt and shorts, and left the house the same way he came in. The children, if not asleep, were hiding. He couldn't see them when he passed their room. "Good. It's a sick world, kiddos."

The five-mile jog back home was invigorating. The wind was at his back. The sun was just starting to rise over the horizon. He felt a hunter's high – like he had just killed a great buck. His mind went to the few good times he had as a child. He remembered his seventh birthday. His father was gone on a business trip, and it was just Ben and his mother to celebrate his birthday. She gave him a brand-new red bicycle for his birthday and baked him a chocolate cake. His mother even fixed him his favorite dinner: spaghetti and meatballs. That night, they stayed up late and watched scary movies together. Two days later, when his father got home, he made his wife return the bicycle.

"It's too much money. We can't afford it, Janie."

CHAPTER 3
MASON CHASE

Booger's police scanner went off at 6 am. A double murder had taken place in Southern Hills, a shocking scandal that would soon be blasted throughout the area on KY3 and all the local media outlets. He got in his Corvette and raced to the neighborhood, but yellow crime tape prevented him from entering the crime scene. Booger had worked with the police on numerous occasions to help solve crimes, mostly cold cases, but that wasn't going to happen this time.

"You can't come in," Sargent Willard Barnaby said when he spotted Booger at the scene.

"Was it the same guy that raped and murdered the woman on the south side of town last week?" Booger asked.

"No comment," the sergeant responded. "I can't talk to you about this Booger. Captain's orders."

"Come on, Willard. Just tell me if the M.O. is the same. Tell me if we've got a serial killer in Springfield. I'm not a reporter here. I'm an investigator like you."

This made Willard pause. "No, I'm sorry, Booger. I can't say a word, and nobody else is going to talk to you about this case either."

That statement told Booger a lot. It told him that

the police didn't have a clue who the maniac was behind these murders. It told him there was a psychopath loose in Springfield, and the only chance there was of catching him was if he made a mistake.

Booger watched from behind the police tape as two bodies were carried out of the house. Twenty minutes later, two detectives emerged from the home. Booger recognized one of them. Detective Trevor Hollister was a seasoned detective. With twenty-five years on the Springfield police force, he was easily the most seasoned detective.

"Trevor," Booger shouted, "can I have a word?"

Trevor walked over to the police tape. The detective looked older than his fifty-two years. Police work had eroded the young, energetic detective that Booger used to know. He was worn out, on the downside of a brilliant career. His face was wrinkled, hardened. His hair was gray. He was a tall, thin man who looked like he didn't know how to smile. He wasn't the same man who used to sit with him at Joe's Diner and have a cup of coffee before going to work. They were friends back then, some twenty years ago, but that had all changed with time. Booger didn't know how or why their relationship had soured, but it had. They rarely spoke anymore.

"Booger, you should leave," Trevor said in a matter-of-fact tone. "There is nothing I can say to you."

"Come on, Trevor, just tell me if this was the same psychopath that struck on the southside last week. Tell me if we have a serial killer loose in Springfield."

"No comment, Booger. Now get out of here."

Booger did leave, but not because he was told to. He left because he had all the information he was going to get – and all the information he needed. The police weren't saying anything about the crime, which meant they thought it was likely the two crimes were connected. It told him that these murders were just the beginning and that the police had no clue who the madman was. If this was obviously unrelated, Willard or Trevor should have let him know because they'd want to dispel the notion of a serial killer on the streets. They'd want to show that they weren't worried.

Thirty minutes later, Booger pulled his red Corvette into a parking space at what he liked to refer to as his "headquarters." Booger's home and office were all one facility and had been built and rebuilt at great expense. Some early investments in Walmart had allowed the private investigator a great deal of freedom. He unlocked the front door and walked up the two flights of steps to his third-floor office. Rose was waiting inside.

"I baked you some blueberry muffins. Would you like one and a cup of coffee?"

"Sure, thanks, sweetie. By the way, happy anniversary."

"Oh, you remembered," Rose said, giving her husband a gentle kiss.

"Of course. It's been fifteen months today."

The newlyweds had known each other for nearly forty years. Rose was a server at a greasy-spoon diner. Booger was a customer. They became friends and the friendship slowly grew until they finally married.

"Should I expect some flowers?"

"Maybe," Booger responded.

Every monthly anniversary was the same. Flowers first, then dinner at George's Steakhouse. That was where Rose was working, just before Booger finally proposed to her. The flowers were roses, his wife's favorite, and the flower she was named after. Rose loved roses. Booger had brought her a dozen roses on her birthday for years – long before they were a couple. Now she got them once a month and on every special occasion. Booger was cheap, so he often would complain about the prices to the florists, but always buy them regardless of the price. He believed in sparing no expense for his wife.

The retired sheriff took his coffee and muffin and went into his office, where he would sit in his recliner behind the fine oak desk and read the newspaper for the next hour. Booger was a creature of habit. This was the quiet time he cherished, and Rose always honored. She would never disturb her husband before he'd had his coffee and read his paper. This was his church. His meditation time.

Rose slipped quietly into the office a couple of times to refill his coffee, but she never said a word during that time.

"Rose," Booger yelled once his meditation time was over. "What's on the schedule today?"

Booger often started his workday with that same question, and Rose nearly always responded with "Nothing. Booger. We have nothing on the schedule today."

Booger's schedule was almost always free. Sometimes, there might be a doctor's appointment or some errand that needed to be run, but very rarely was there anything business-related that needed attention. His private detective agency had very few clients over the last several years, and that allowed him to work on cases he wanted to work on. He was an investigator at heart, so he tried to regularly put some work into the area's unsolved cases, but days where anything ever needed to get done were the exception.

"Rose, do you know the Freeman family or the Henry family?"

"No, I don't believe I do."

"Well, the police scanner that went off this morning was about the murders of Mr. and Mrs. Freeman, and the Henry case was a murder that happened last week."

"Do you think they are related?"

"I don't know for sure. The police wouldn't tell me anything which leads me to believe they are."

"Okay, so maybe someone they knew killed them?"

"I don't think so. I think it might have been a complete stranger."

"A robbery gone bad?"

"No. I doubt it was a robbery."

"What then?"

"I think we have a serial killer loose in Springfield."

"Oh my. What makes you think that?"

"It's what the police didn't say. When I mentioned serial killer twice to two of the cops on the scene, neither denied it. I don't think they know for certain, but I do think they are worried that the killer may have just got started."

It was at that moment that the front doorbell rang. Booger looked at his video surveillance camera and pointed to the area around the front door. An older man, about sixty, tall, large build, was standing at the door.

"Can I help you?" Rose said over the intercom just to the right of the front door.

"Yes, I'm Mason Chase. I'm a detective from the Wichita Police Department. I would like to speak to Booger McClain."

Rose shot a look to Booger. "Can I see your badge, detective? Just hold it up to the video camera just to the right of the front door."

The detective, a bit surprised by the level of scrutiny, pulled out his badge as asked and held it up.

"Thank you, detective," Rose said as she buzzed the front door to open.

"Booger's office is on the third floor. You can take the elevator or stairs. It's your choice."

A couple of minutes later, the detective was inside Booger's reception room.

"Can I get you a cup of coffee?" Rose said with a smile.

"Sure, that would be nice," he replied. "I take mine black."

"Good, that's the right answer because we don't have sugar or creamer. Ha!" Rose said with a hearty laugh.

"Oh, okay," Mason said, not sure what to think.

"Actually, we do have sugar and creamer, but I'm more of a coffee purist myself," she said as she poured him a cup. "Booger will be with you in just a moment."

"Oh, umm, sure."

One minute later, Booger walked in, extended his hand for a handshake, and said, "Booger McClain here. What brings you from Wichita?"

"Hello, Mr. McClain, I'm Mason Chase."

"And you're a detective with the Wichita Police Department. I saw you on the monitor. I tell ya, let's move to my office and find out why you drove six hours to meet me."

"Sure." Once they rounded the corner, Mason Chase could see a wall of video monitors and wondered to himself just what he'd walked into. "Well, to answer your question: officially, I'm on vacation. I'm bad about doing that, so I've built up my PTO, and now I'm taking a month off. Unofficially, I am bad at taking vacations, and I believe you have a serial killer hunting women in Springfield."

"Oh good, you're right to the point," Booger said, noticing the detective was getting ready to take his first sip of coffee. "Wait!"

"What?" Mason said, alarmed, looking at his cup.

Booger reached into his desk and pulled out a half-full bottle of rye whiskey. "You may want to put a little of this in your drink before you take a sip."

The detective looked puzzled.

"Trust me," Booger replied pouring a shot full in

the coffee.

Mason took a sip, shook his head, and took another sip. "This coffee tastes a little bit like motor oil, but the whiskey takes the edge off."

"Yes, that's the idea. My wife, God love her, thinks I need triple-strength coffee in the morning to wake me up. I don't need it, never have, but I don't want to spoil her fun."

"Well, sure," Mason said with a chuckle, still unsure what to think about his new surroundings.

"Now, you were mentioning that a serial killer might be in Springfield, detective."

"Yes, about twelve years ago, we had a serial killer in Wichita that took the lives of eight women and four men. His name was Wade Collins. I was the lead detective on the case, and I was getting close. That's when he came for me and attacked my girlfriend. I shot him, but he got away and jumped into a lake. We assumed he drowned, but his body was never recovered. Shortly thereafter, he left me a message to let me know he was still alive."

"What was the message?"

"Cigarette butts."

"What?"

"Cigarette butts. Over a dozen of them were left under a tall oak tree just outside the cabin where he attacked my girlfriend. You see, Collins was a chain smoker. The butts were fresh. I've always believed they were his way of telling me that he was still alive. That he was still out there."

"Okay, you've got my attention."

"A few weeks later, my girlfriend was killed in a car accident, but it wasn't an accident. Her brake lines had been cut. It was Collins. I'm certain of it."

Booger sat back in his chair, opened his desk drawer, and pulled out two fine stogies. "Want one?" he asked.

"Sure, thanks."

Booger handed him one and a book of matches. Then he lit one himself and took several long drags before talking again. "It's been twelve years since that happened, right?"

"Yes, that's right."

"Why do you suppose a serial killer would stop killing for twelve years and then suddenly resume again?"

"I don't know. Maybe he was in prison, or maybe he found religion, or maybe he found love. I really don't know, but whatever the reason, he's back to killing again."

"How can you be certain it's the same man and he's in Springfield?"

"A diary."

"What?"

"His mother's diary. He was very close to his mother, and she kept a diary. The mother was in a terrible, loveless marriage. Her husband used to beat her. He was an abusive alcoholic. Wade was only a young child at the time and unable to protect her. But one day, his father nearly killed his mother. Wade tried to stop him, and the father took out his anger on his son. The father chased him through the house to the basement stairs, where he fell to his death. It seems Mother pushed him down those stairs."

"Why do you think that?"

"It was written in her diary. The mother confessed in the diary to killing her husband."

"So, where's this diary now?"

"I've got it. Inside it, the mother talks about her life after her husband's death. She went through a series of failed relationships, mostly with married men who made her promises and then went back to their wives. Each failed relationship drove her further into depression until finally, she committed suicide."

"Okay, so that explains Wade's hatred for cheating married men. But why does he attack women?"

"I believe he attacks women who remind him of his mother. Down deep, he has a real hatred for his mother. I don't know why. Maybe a psychiatrist can give more insight. But I suspect it has something to do with the period of her life after the husband's death. She was a very lonely woman. She needed a man in her life, and she went looking for one in bars. That's where she met so many married men. Wade's mother would dress up in her favorite red dress and go looking in bars for a man, any man, just someone to be with, to take the loneliness away for a little while. It's all in her diary," Mason said, now excited to be sharing what he knows and speaking fast. "Janie was a very attractive woman. She had no trouble getting men. But they were always the wrong ones – married men, men who used her and then left. With every failed relationship, Wade was left to deal with the deepening depression that his mother would go through. He would nurse her back to some sort of normality, and then she would go looking for another man. After her death, Wade found the diary and began seeking revenge on the men that drove his mother to commit suicide."

"But, again, what about the women? You said he murdered eight women and four men. Were all the women like his mother in some way?"

"Yes. Sorry, I'm a bit excited, I suppose. Most people I've tried to talk to about this case aren't so interested. Wade seemed to attack a certain type of woman. Provocative women. Women in red dresses. Mothers."

"So, what makes you think Wade is in Springfield?"

"I don't think he is here. I know he is here."

"How can you be sure? There have only been two attacks, and one happened last night. You couldn't possibly even know about it yet."

"No, I didn't know. Tell me, was the latest murder victim a woman or a man?"

"A woman and a man. There've been two attacks, but three people have died. A couple died last night."

"Well, actually, there's been a couple of other murders," Mason said. "Both have happened in the last year."

"Oh wow," Rose said over the intercom, to Mason's surprise. "Those might have happened when we were in Arkansas, Booger."

"You're right, Rose," Booger said to the speaker. "That explains why the police have been so tight-lipped."

"Plus, not everyone likes you," Rose said through the grainy intercom with a snort.

"Springfield cops know they have a problem. That's why I am here," Mason said. "Collins just recently started murdering women again. I tried to talk to my boss in Wichita about it, but he wants me to let it go. As far as the chief is concerned, Wade Collins drowned a dozen years ago. So, I'm here unofficially. I'm here on vacation. But I'm telling you, unless we're able to stop him, he'll keep on killing."

"What do you mean, you and I?"

"Well, Booger McClain, you have quite a reputation for uncovering the truth. I figured you would want to help me find Wade Collins and stop him from killing any more people."

"Why me? Why not contact the police?"

"Because the police won't be able to stop him. Not without proof. They have rules and certain procedures they must follow. You know it's true. And Collins knows this. He's too smart for them. The second they come after him, he'll run and never be caught. You and I have no rules or procedures that we have to follow. We can do whatever it takes to stop this monster."

"Oh, Booger, this one sounds interesting," Rose said, as she entered Booger's office. "You gotta let me help. This Wade guy sounds like a real sicko."

"You met Rose, right?" Booger asked the detective with a knowing smile.

CHAPTER 4
THE SALESMAN

Coleman Brothers, Josh and Joseph, had inherited their family's car dealership when their father, Jack, died of a heart attack at the age of fifty-five. Josh was a senior in high school then. His older brother had graduated from Missouri State University and was already working in the family business. Their mother, Cristine, was thirteen years younger than their father and handled the bookkeeping for the business at the time.

Retired now, Christine met Jack twenty-five years earlier at the Shady Inn Restaurant, where she was a server. Their attraction was instant. He was well-heeled, dressed in a suit, and with plenty of money to spend. She was eighteen, a high-school dropout who grew up on the poor side of town.

Jack was her ticket out of a life she didn't particularly want. She became pregnant three months after they met. They married a month later. Their marriage was turbulent at times. Christine liked to drink. Over the years, she was a frequent attendee at local AA meetings. But sobriety never stuck. Time and again, she would turn and return to the bottle when life got tough. And it was always tough.

When she went back to drinking, Christine often

partied at Terry's Tavern, a seedy bar on the northwest side of town. Jack would find her there, many times in the arms of a stranger. He always brought her home and forgave her.

Jack was a good man. He never blamed his wife, only her addiction, for her indiscretions.

When he died, he left the business to Christine and his two sons, divided equally among the three. Today, Coleman Brothers Chevrolet is one of the largest dealerships in southwest Missouri.

Joseph managed the business, and Josh was a gifted mechanic who oversaw the service department. They had over thirty employees. One of those was Ben Sawyers – a man their mother asked him to hire. He was a salesman. He wasn't particularly good at his job; he sold just enough cars to pay his bills and keep from being fired.

One of the perks of working for the dealership was always having a new car to drive. That was of particular interest to Ben.

As luck would have it, on one recent sunny day, a couple walked into the dealership at the exact time it was Ben's turn in the sales queue. His attention went instantly to the young woman wearing a maroon dress. She was a platinum blonde, shy, and sported fancy new sunglasses. She seemed to not want to be noticed, and she wasn't wearing a ring on her finger, which was notable because the gentleman in his sixties that she was with wore a wedding band.

Ben figured them out instantly. The man was a

sugar daddy, married to a woman he didn't particularly love anymore. The woman, in her mid to late twenties, was single and looking to land a man of means. He had made a promise to leave his wife someday. But someday never came. The new car was a present to her to keep her happy just a little bit longer.

He paid cash for the car, gave a false name, and put the title of the car in his girlfriend's name. She was easy to find. Her address was on the paperwork, an upper-end apartment near Sequiota Park. Her sugar daddy was a little harder to find. Ben sat in his car and waited outside the woman's apartment every night for nearly a week before he spotted the man in his black Cadillac pulling into a parking space outside the apartment complex. He followed them to Red Lobster. Then to a wine bar, and finally back to the apartment. The man was inside for nearly two hours. When he left the apartment, Ben followed him. As he hoped, the sugar daddy drove home. Henry Keller was his name. He lived in a nice two-story home off Cox Road south of the James River Freeway. Henry and his wife lived alone. Their two grown children had left home nearly twenty years ago.

Henry was a personal injury lawyer. His wife, Peggy, was a homemaker. From all appearances, they had a happy marriage.

On a stormy Tuesday night, Henry called his wife to tell her he would be working late. When he hung up, Henry left the office, stopped at a flower shop, and purchased a dozen roses. Then, he went to a liquor store and purchased two bottles of champagne before picking up Cashew Chicken.

Soon, he was at the apartment of his girlfriend. It was a night of passion, much of which Ben saw from an open bedroom window.

That window became the stalker's entrance into the apartment after both lovers had fallen asleep. He subdued the man first, tied him up, and gagged him before doing the same to the girlfriend. Henry was forced to watch as the maniac took his girlfriend. He strangled her first. Then, he turned to the lawyer, who was desperately trying to negotiate through his gag. It was no use. A knife slowly slit his throat, but it wasn't deep enough to kill him instantly. Ben wanted him to suffer. Slowly, he bled out. It took him over twenty minutes to die. Ben sat in a chair next to the bed and watched until there was no movement.

Killing, it seemed, was the only thing that gave him peace. It was the only thing that held Ben's demons at bay. At the car dealership or in everyday interactions with people, Ben was awkward, irritable, and prone to daydreams and delusions of grandeur. But if he was killing someone he considered bad, he was making the world a better place. If only for him. It gave him a sense of control.

With Henry dead, Ben packed his kill kit and left through the front door. It was 3 am.

Peggy was frantic when her husband didn't come home that night. He had come home in the wee hours of the morning on numerous occasions, but he had never stayed out all night. She first called the office, hoping he had just fallen asleep there. Then, she called the police to report him missing.

Peggy would learn the fate of her husband three days later. The odor coming from the apartment was overwhelming. It was a maintenance worker who first went inside and discovered the bodies. A policeman would visit Peggy a few hours later to give her the news.

Booger heard about the murders on the police scanner in his office. He stopped and picked up Mason Chase from the lobby of the Drury Inn about thirty minutes later. Together, they drove to the crime scene.

The area around the apartment was cornered off with police tape. But from a distance, Booger could see crime scene investigators taking pictures of the open window and an area outside in the grass where there were numerous cigarette butts.

"It's him," Mason said. "The cigarette butts, the open window, the Wichita Maniac has struck again."

When KY3 came on at 10 pm that night, the two murders were their top story. "A serial killer has once again struck in Springfield, but this time, police say they have a major clue."

The clue was not disclosed by the police, but it was reported as collected, which certainly sparked Booger and Mason's attention. That night after midnight, they quietly broke into the apartment where the couple were murdered. Removing the police tape from the door was easy. A small tear in it would be retaped when the two detectives left the apartment. Unlocking the door proved a little more difficult. The small metal tool that Booger brought took several tries before the lock finally released. Inside, they used flashlights to scour every inch of the apartment. The blood-soaked bed spoke to the brutality of the crime.

Inside a drawer in the nightstand in the bedroom, Mason found a book of matches from Terry's Tavern. In a desk drawer near the entranceway to the apartment were the keys to the victim's new Chevy Camaro.

After leaving the apartment, the two detectives wandered the parking lot in search of the victim's car. Not knowing what it looked like, the only way to find it was by pushing the alarm on the key. That would guide them to the car, but it might also wake up sleeping residents. It was a chance they needed to take. When the alarm went off, the lights to the car flashed. They had what they were looking for.

Inside the car, in the glove compartment, they found the sales contract for the new car. Along with it, they found the business card of the salesman who sold the victim the car. His name was Ben Sawyers. The victim's name, which had not been released on the news earlier that evening, was Madison Goans, Booger discovered from the sales contract.

Less than five minutes after getting inside the car, Booger and Mason heard the police sirens in the background.

"Someone must have called the police," Mason said. The two detectives hurried back to Booger's car and sped out of the parking lot just as they saw two police cars approaching the parking lot from the other side.

"Damn, that was close," Mason said.

They both laughed. Booger felt an easy kinship with Mason. Booger had been a sheriff before, and it felt like he had a partner suddenly. It was a good feeling.

"Do you think the salesman knows something?" Mason asked on the drive back to his hotel.

"I doubt it," Booger said. "But it's worth checking out. The date on the contract was nearly three weeks ago. Chances are he has nothing to do with the case. But a lead is a lead."

"What about the matches? Do you know anything about Terry's Tavern?"

"It's a small place on the north side of town. We'll check it out too."

"I just wish we had a picture of the victim to show."

"You mean like this one," Mason said, pulling out a small photo from his jacket pocket.

"Where'd you get that?"

"In the desk drawer in her bedroom. It's not a particularly good photo, done in one of those mall photo booths I assume, but it will do."

Booger looked over the photo. "Damn, she was an attractive young woman."

"Yeah, well, somehow she got the attention of our psychopath."

Booger dropped Mason off at the Drury Inn a few minutes later before heading home. "Get some rest. I'll pick you up at 10 am. We have work to do."

Rose was just waking up when Booger arrived home.

"Long night?"

"Yeah."

"Did you find anything?"

"A book of matches."

"Good. You can always use them."

"Funny."

"How do they help solve your crime?"

"I don't know yet. You ever hear of a place called Terry's Tavern?"

"Hmm. No."

"That's the name on the matches."

"So?"

"So, it's a seedy little bar on Kearney. It's the type of place you'd expect to find hookers, not a classy woman like the one murdered."

"How do you know she's classy?"

"I don't really. I'm just guessing. But based on her lifestyle, her sugar daddy was certainly trying to make her classy."

"Maybe it didn't take. Or maybe she had two sides to her, sort of like a split personality."

"Maybe."

"What else did you find?"

"Nothing, really.

"Madison, that's the dead woman's name, purchased a new car just a few weeks earlier. Or, more than likely, her sugar daddy purchased the car. And there was a sales receipt in the glove compartment. It had the name of the salesman on it."

"So, how's that a clue?"

"It probably isn't, but it tells us one place she was several days ago. It's worth talking to the salesman."

"So, you're assuming that someone she encountered in recent days may have killed her?"

"Not just someone. I think sometime in the last several days, she came in close contact with our serial killer."

"Well, okay. So, when are you going to the bar and the car dealership?"

"Today."

"I want to come."

"No."

"Why?"

"Because we don't need you there." This changed the temperature in the room. Booger sensed instantly that this was the wrong thing to say.

"Dammit, Booger. I've told you I wanted to be more involved, and now you're just going to brush me aside because you've met a new cop friend."

It was true. Rose had helped on several cases and made it clear to her husband that she felt she brought "a new perspective to each one."

"No, it's not like that," Booger said with a wrinkle in his chin.

"Well, of course it is. And I'm coming anyway. If you're going to a seedy bar frequented by hookers, I'm coming to keep an eye on you."

"No," he said softly, but his wife had already turned away. He knew now that she was on the case, too. He loved her, but he couldn't help but think this would complicate things.

At 10 am, Booger McClain pulled up to the Drury Inn entrance. Mason Chase came out of the hotel carrying two cups of coffee.

"Hi, Rose," Mason said, seeing Rose in the seat next to Booger.

"Hello, Mason," Rose replied as she stepped out of the car and got into the backseat. "I'll let you boys sit upfront so you can discuss your little plans."

"I'm sorry," he said, sensing a thickness in the air. "I only got two cups of coffee. I didn't know you were coming, or I would have got three."

"No problem. I brought a thermos of coffee from home."

Mason sat down in the passenger seat and handed Booger a cup of coffee.

"Umm. No thanks, Buddy," he said, pointing to his own thermos.

"Well, okay," Mason said, knowing he'd missed something between them. "I can drink both."

CHAPTER 5
FORMAL GREETINGS

Rose wasn't new to investigating. She had helped Booger many times in small ways and large. She had worked closely, for example, with the prostitutes at the Shadow Valley Trailer Park to help uncover what had happened to the Trussle women in northwest Arkansas. She'd adjusted her wedding plans and sacrificed, temporarily at least, her honeymoon as her husband pursued what had happened to the three boys of Hannibal. She had her car bugged and narrowly escaped a devastating fire at the office when Booger was trying to solve the three missing women's case. In her mind, the days of being a passive participant were over.

Still, Booger felt this was different. He and Mason were chasing a psychopath, and not just any psychopath, but one that had likely killed dozens of women. The detective's protective nature couldn't help but worry about his wife's involvement this time. He wouldn't fight her on joining them today, but he would look for opportunities to keep her on the sidelines. To keep her safe. And, if he was honest, to keep his new cop friend to himself.

"So, what's first today?" Mason asked his two companions in the car.

"The first stop is at the Coleman Brothers car dealership to talk to the salesman, one of the last people to see Madison alive," Booger said.

Mason and Rose nodded in agreement. The car ride was quiet, with each of them lost in thought. As the three detectives walked into the dealership, the receptionist behind the desk gave a warm smile.

"May I help you?" she asked.

"Yes, we are here to see Ben Sawyers. Is he available?" Rose asked.

"Let me check," she replied.

"Ben Sawyers, you are wanted at the receptionist's desk," she said into the intercom.

A minute later, a thin, balding man in his late forties appeared at the receptionist's desk.

"Hello, I'm Ben. How can I help you?" he asked.

A cold chill went down Mason Chase's back.

"Mr. Sawyers, we'd like to ask you a few questions about a recent customer of yours," Booger replied.

"Are you with the police?"

"No."

"Okay, follow me."

A few seconds later, they were seated on the other side of Ben's desk.

"Here we are. So, what can I help you with?" he asked.

"You had a customer a couple of weeks ago, a young woman and an older gentleman who purchased a new Chevy Camaro from you. I believe the man paid for the car and it was titled in the young woman's name:

Madison Goans."

"Was?"

"Yes, she was murdered a couple of days ago," Booger responded.

"Oh, my. Murdered by the older gentleman?"

"No, he was murdered too."

"Oh, wow. This is the first I've heard of it. I've gotten in the habit of avoiding the news. That's a real shame. I do remember those two. But what does that have to do with the car they purchased?"

"Maybe nothing," Booger responded. "But you were one of the last people to see the couple together."

"That was a couple of weeks ago, right? Surely, they were seen by quite a few people after coming here."

"Likely, that's right. However, you are the only one who we know for sure saw them so far," Booger said, now pivoting towards Mason. "Ben, this is Mason Chase. He's a detective with the Wichita Police Department. I'm Booger McClain – a former sheriff and a P.I., and this is my wife, Rose."

"I'm a P.I., too," Rose added.

"We have reason to believe the person responsible could be a serial killer, and we were wondering if there was anything unusual about the couple that you might remember?"

Booger hoped this more formal introduction might help the salesman take them seriously. He also hoped saying that they were looking for a serial killer might garner a significant reaction – something that would be telling. It didn't. Ben was stone-faced.

"No, other than he was much older and looked to be doing well for himself, if you know what I mean. She was young – pretty, I guess. I sensed he was somewhat of a sugar daddy to her, but that's none of my business. They seemed to get along well, and nothing seemed out of the ordinary."

"You said she was young and attractive. Did you notice anyone following her or them? Was there anyone paying unusual attention to the couple?" Mason asked.

Ben seemed to watch the detective closely for a moment before answering plainly: "No, not that I noticed."

"How long have you worked here? Are you from Springfield?" Rose interjected.

"Oh, I've been here about a year and a half." Before anyone could respond, Ben had a question of his own. "Do you have a picture of him?"

"Who?" Booger asked.

"The serial killer."

Booger was going to say something before Mason coughed gently to let him know he'd answer. Mason looked directly into Ben's eyes and said, "No."

There was a long pause before Ben said, "I understand. Well, I'm sorry I couldn't be of much help to you."

"No problem," Booger said, looking at Mason to see if there was anything else that needed to be asked. A simple nod indicated he was ready to move on. "We're just following up on leads. If you do remember anything, please give me a call," the detective said, handing Ben a business card.

The trio stood up, but before they began to walk out of the dealership, Rose noticed a bowl of matches. "Are those your matches?" she asked Ben, pointing to an adjacent desk.

"No, that's our owner's desk. Christine. She's retired and barely ever here, but she collects matches from different places."

"Oh well, I smoke stogies from time to time," Booger said, going straight for the bowl. "Do you mind?"

"No. She's said customers are welcome to them," Ben said. "I don't smoke myself."

Booger noticed that about half of the matches had Terry's Tavern written on them.

"Did you used to?" Mason asked Ben. "Smoke?"

"Never. I'm a jogger, and those two things don't go well together."

And with that, the three detectives left.

When they got out to the car, Mason said, "That's him. I'm certain of it. That's Wade Collins. His looks have changed, but I'm certain he's the Wichita killer."

"Shit," Rose replied.

"What makes you certain he is?" Booger asked.

"It's his eyes. I'll never forget the look in his eyes the last time I saw him."

"But it's been well over ten years. Isn't it possible you're wrong?"

"It's possible. But I doubt it. When I first saw him, chills shot down my back. I'm pretty certain he's the psychopath."

"Did you think he recognized you?"

"I can't be sure. At first, yes. But then he spoke with such ease. It should have scared him that I was here."

"But you think it's him?"

"Yes. Absolutely."

Booger nodded his head. "Okay, then we need to notify the police."

Together, they went to the West Battlefield police station. Booger reasoned that with a pair of recent southside murders, the detective in charge would be there instead of at the downtown station. Within minutes, they were introduced to Charlie Johnson. Charlie Johnson had been a Springfield detective for nearly twenty years. He was a heavy-set chain smoker with balding hair and a big beer gut. He was named lead detective for the recent murders suspected of being committed by a serial killer.

"Detective," Booger replied. "You need to look into Wade Collins, a salesman at Coleman Brothers. He goes by the name of Ben Sawyers. We think he could be your serial killer."

"And what makes you think that, Mr. McClain?"

"My friend, Mason Chase, is a detective with the Wichita Police Department. I'll let him explain."

"Detective, we had a serial killer in Wichita about twelve years ago. He murdered several young women. He nearly murdered my girlfriend. She barely escaped from him. I chased him down and shot him. He fell into the lake, and we assumed he was killed, but his body was never found. I think he escaped to Springfield and, for some reason, stopped killing for eleven or twelve years until recently, when he began again. And he's living under another name now."

The detective began to laugh. "I'm sorry," he responded. "I don't mean to be disrespectful. It's tough times for us cops, and I want to take you at your word, but if you are a detective, you should know how that sounds. It's real loose, detective," Charlie said, trying to show Mason respect by calling him detective in return. "Why, if he survived, would he come to Springfield? Does he have family here?"

"Well, not that I know of?"

"Okay, why, if he's a serial killer, would he stop for a dozen years? Did he have a change of heart?"

"I don't know. It's possible he moved out of Wichita and continued elsewhere before moving here."

"Sure, sure. It just doesn't make any sense. Besides, how'd you get the name Ben Sawyers anyway? And how'd you know he was selling cars? You boys didn't happen to be over at the dead woman's apartment last night, did you?"

Booger and Mason looked at each other with a quiet alarm. "No detective, what makes you say that?" Mason said.

"Oh well, you know, someone broke into the apartment and the victim's new car last night. Thought you boys and lady might have been doing something that will land you in a lot of trouble. Surely you wouldn't be interfering in a live investigation," Charlie said, looking directly at Booger.

"No detective. That wasn't us," Booger said softly,

not able to look the detective straight in the eye.

"Ben Sawyers used to be Wade Collins. I'm sure of it," Mason said, feeling a bit desperate to be heard.

"Well, do me a favor and stay out of trouble and stay away from our investigation. I'll look into it, and if we have any evidence that this Ben or Wayne guy is involved, we'll act on it."

"Wade," Mason said.

"Huh?"

"It's Wade Collins."

"Sure," Charlie said.

Trying to forget their disappointing meeting with Charlie Johnson, the three pushed forward and went to Terry's Tavern. They were following that book of matches, their only solid clue. The ride over in Booger's custom three-seat Corvette was largely quiet. Mason felt defeated.

"Don't worry," Rose told him. "If it's him, it's him. We'll figure it out."

He nodded yes.

At the bar, they were greeted quickly.

"Hello, can I get you something to drink?" a barmaid on the downside of fifty asked.

"I'll take a double rye on ice," Booger replied.

"Make that two of them," Mason added.

"Just a Coke for me, please," Rose said.

"Miss, can you tell me if you've seen this woman come in here?" Mason said, pulling out a picture of Madison from his pocket.

"Yes, I've seen her come in several times, usually

with an older woman."

"What did the older woman look like?"

"Classy lady. Tall, thin, long, blond hair, usually wears a red dress," she said, pointing them to a table before disappearing behind the kitchen's double doors.

The trio sat down at the table near the back of the bar. That's when Mason Chase opened up – in part, to tell Booger more about the diary, but also to catch Rose up to speed.

"There was a diary we found at one of the crime scenes – the mother's diary. In it, she admits to pushing her husband down the stairs of their basement, breaking his neck. Janie, Wade's mother, went through a long period of depression after that. He tried to comfort her, but nothing seemed to work. Eventually, she started going out to bars, seedy bars for the most part. She often wore a red dress when she went out. In the bars, she picked up a lot of men, mostly older, married men. She began affairs with them. None of the affairs lasted long or amounted to much of anything, but it made the son very jealous. He looked up to his mother and blamed her for being weak when it came to men. He also blamed the men for cheating on their wives."

Booger and Rose were locked in. They gave Mason their full attention. He continued. "Every affair the mother had ended badly and resulted in her falling into a deeper depression. It was like she was a drug addict and couldn't stop, but she carried a lot of shame with it. Well, that weight only got heavier with time. The son watched as his mother deteriorated until she finally took her own life. That was the catalyst that drove him to murder, seeking out young, attractive women and married men who cheated on their wives. After his mother died, the murdering began. The son was very sick. I think he had a lot of deep-rooted mental issues. The death of his mother seemed to be the straw that broke the camel's back. The writing had been on the wall for many years, even before the family moved to Wichita. When the boy was young, they lived in Park Hills, Missouri – on the east side of the state. You may remember the town because of the famous disappearance of Tina Mae Cooks."

"Oh, my God," Booger interrupted. "I briefly investigated that case when I was with the FBI over thirty years ago."

"Well then, you'll probably remember a kid by the name of Ben Squires. He lived down the block from Tina."

"Yes, I remember him. He was implicated as one of three boys that may have abducted her. They were driving an old beat-up station wagon, one similar to a station wagon owned by Ben's mother back then. I was certain the three boys abducted Tina the last night she was seen and drove away with her, but we were never able to prove anything. The Squires family moved away a short time later, as I remember."

"Yes, well, I believe they moved to Wichita and changed their names. That young man became the Wichita serial killer."

CHAPTER 6
FIVE BLOCKS FROM HOME

Norman Rockwell's small-town America was a good way to describe Park Hills. Nestled in the foothills of the St. Francois mountains in the northeastern Ozarks, this blip on the map was a picture-perfect reflection of small-town life. This was old Missouri. Old rural Missouri, where the lead mines used to hire anyone who didn't move north to St. Louis. Things move at a relaxed pace in Park Hills. It was a place where God and family were much more important than the accumulation of wealth and creature comforts. Neighbors looked out for neighbors, and everyone knew everyone else. Or do they?

The people of Park Hills were content with the quiet grace and humble lifestyle that was reminiscent of Mayberry, USA, in the 60s. Teenagers cruised the streets at night. Children walked to the ice cream parlor and rode their bicycles wherever they wanted. It was a safe place to raise a family. Or, at least, it used to be.

Nothing was completely safe, and the peaceful tranquility of Park Hills was changed forever on August 12, 1989. That was the evening that Tina Mae Cooks disappeared.

Tina, thirteen, disappeared less than five blocks from home at around 11 pm that night while riding her bike to see her boyfriend, T.J. Moore. She rode her bike late at night countless times before. After all, Park Hills was safe, and neighbors looked out for neighbors.

But this night was different. There was a darkness in the air. Like countless times before, Tina rode her bike down the city streets in the south-center part of town, past the ice cream parlor to an area near the First Baptist Church. That's where she met up with her boyfriend, T.J., and his best friend, Chad Morgansen. T.J. and Chad had been best friends since first grade. T.J. was the leader; Chad was the follower. T.J. was outgoing and popular. He and Tina were nearly exact opposites. Maybe that's what attracted them to each other. Tina was a bit introverted. Attractive and smart, she was very independent and felt comfortable being self-reliant. They had known each other for many years, but Tina had not been attracted to T.J. until recent months. She had always seen him as a little too outgoing, a little too popular, and someone out of her league. At that age, children were hyper-aware of their social hierarchy. Seventh grade, however, changed everything. Tina was growing up, and T.J. took notice. They became friends at first and then their friendship blossomed into something more.

That fateful night, they talked for a few minutes about school and their plans for the weekend. At about 10:45 pm, she said goodnight to T.J. and Chad and began to ride her bike back home to get back before her 11 pm curfew. A minute after she left, T.J. spotted the old station wagon driving slowly down the road. Tina was only about a block away when the station wagon caught up to her and stopped. T.J. would later say there was an exchange of words between Tina and someone in the station wagon. Then, he said, a boy got out of the car and grabbed her off her bicycle. He dragged her to the backseat of the car, and then it sped off.

It happened so fast, just a few seconds that T.J. and Chad didn't have time to get to her. Even if they had, it was doubtful they could have prevented her abduction. There were three abductors, they said, all older.

Her bike was found lying on the ground near her family's church. There was no sign of her or evidence that anything sinister had happened beyond what the boys had seen – three men, Tina being grabbed quickly, and then her screaming from the back seat. People nearby heard the screams, but no one thought anything sinister was happening. After all, this was Park Hills.

Deputy Mike Difficile was the first policeman on the scene. He responded to a call from Tina's parents when their daughter did not return from her bike ride.

Other than Tina's bicycle lying on the ground, Difficile found nothing out of the ordinary. Tina Mae had simply disappeared. Witnesses' reports of the station wagon and the three men inside varied.

Interviews with T.J., Chad, and several neighbors who heard the girl's screams for help put the investigation on a more urgent track. T.J. and Chad were eyewitnesses to the abduction. Their depiction of the three abductors was vague, but their description of the battered station wagon was helpful to police. Others would come forward to report seeing the station wagon cruising the streets earlier that night. One eyewitness was certain he saw the station wagon leave Park Hills and head north on Hwy. 67 toward St. Louis.

No one reported seeing the station wagon after it left town, nor did anyone ever report seeing the station wagon return. It became a mystery where the car went and whatever happened to the thirteen-year-old girl.

Booger T. McClain was an FBI field agent with the St. Louis bureau at the time. When it became apparent that Tina had been abducted, the FBI entered the case, and Booger became the field agent in charge. To say he was received well by the locals would be a mischaracterization. Booger drove into Park Hills three days after the disappearance. The sight of a six-foot, three-inch man wearing a white Stetson cowboy hat, rattlesnake cowboy boots, and a large silver belt buckle in the shape of the state map of Missouri may have been a little too much for the conservative townspeople. He was an outsider.

Booger's first stop was the sheriff's office to introduce himself and to offer the FBI's assistance with the case. The offer was purely symbolic. The FBI was getting involved whether the sheriff wanted it or not. It was obvious at the time that Tina had been kidnapped, and that was a crime that fell within the FBI's jurisdiction. Offering assistance was just a matter of common courtesy.

"I'm looking for Sheriff Parras," Booger told the officer at the desk.

"And you are?"

"Booger McClain, St. Louis bureau of the FBI," he

said, showing his badge.

"He's in his office. I'll tell him you're here."

A couple of minutes later, the officer returned. "You can go on in. He's waiting for you."

The sheriff's office was small, a tiny rectangular room about the size of a large living room with two desks, a table with a coffee pot, and a small office tucked away in one corner. That was Sheriff Parras' office.

Booger knocked on the door and entered. "Hello, sheriff. I'm Booger McClain with the FBI."

Parras stared at him for what seemed like a minute or two then he smiled. "Boy, you certainly don't look like an FBI agent."

"So, what do you think an FBI agent ought to look like?"

"Suit, tie, polished shoes."

"I'm what they call the new breed of FBI agents. We dress like everyday people."

"People around here who have jobs dress like they have jobs."

Booger had not made a great first impression. "Sheriff, I'm here to investigate the Tina Mae Cook's disappearance."

"Boy, we don't need any help from the FBI."

"Not offering help, sheriff. The FBI is taking over the investigation. Kidnapping falls under our jurisdiction so this is pretty much a courtesy call to let you know we're taking control. I'd appreciate it if you'd provide us your case files and any evidence you've dug up so far."

"Boy you got a lot of nerve. This is my town, and

Tina is one of our people. I don't give a damn what jurisdiction you say the crime falls under, we are going to continue our investigation, and if you know what's good for you, you'll stay out of our way."

"That sounds like a threat, sheriff."

"If it looks like a pig and smells like a pig, it probably is a pig."

"Sheriff, I don't want to get into a pissing match with you, but I want those files and any evidence you have, and I want it right away."

"Boy, that just ain't going to happen. First off, there ain't no case files. We've got notes, and the rest of what we know is in my head, and you sure as hell aren't getting that unless you're some sort of hypnotist."

"Sheriff why don't you just make it easier on both of us and give me a copy of the notes you have on the case."

"Boy, are you hard of hearing? I told you that I ain't giving you crap, so why don't you just get the hell outta Dodge and go right back where you came from."

"That's another thing, sheriff, I don't like being called boy. The next time you call me it, I'm going to shove your tongue back in your throat and make you swallow that word."

"That's it, son. You're under arrest for threatening an officer."

"Roy, handcuff this son of a bitch," the sheriff said to his deputy standing next to him.

Booger McClain had been in town less than thirty minutes and had managed to get himself locked up. A phone call to the FBI field office in St. Louis would result in another agent, Terrance Moffitt, taking a trip to Park Hills with three additional agents. Moffitt was a seasoned field agent with nearly ten years of experience. His boss, Captain Clay Herald, had first assigned Moffitt to the case. It was Terrence Moffitt who recommended Booger. "He's a good old boy from southern Missouri, Captain. I think he'll be able to get information that I might have difficulty getting from the locals."

Now, it was Moffitt's job to clean up whatever mess landed his rookie agent in jail. Captain Herald made it clear that Moffitt was responsible for Booger McClain. Moffitt arrived with a court order to release McClain and another court order to surrender the case files of Tina Mae Cooks along with any evidence.

Booger, new to the St. Louis field office, had met Terry only a few times before, but they had hit it off immediately in the way that best friends sometimes do. He knew him as a straight-shooter, a dedicated agent, and an up-and-comer in the FBI. They had respect for each other.

"Hello, Terry. I'm glad to see you. You going to get me out of this place."

"Yeah, but on one condition."

"What's that?"

"You need to apologize to Sheriff Parras for threatening him."

"It was more of a promise than a threat."

"Either way, you need to apologize."

Booger would apologize to the sheriff, but that

hardly smoothed things over. Booger was on the shit list with Parras, and he was not the type of person to let Booger forget it. They would be enemies from that point forward, and it was he who ultimately got Booger kicked off the case.

Parras had been sheriff of Park Hills for nearly thirty years. He was a hardened old crow who had no tolerance for outsiders. In his mind, the FBI had no business in his town. He wasn't going to cooperate with them if his life depended on it.

The heavy-set, gray-haired, balding Parras reminded Booger of a bulldog. He was short, stocky, and full of bite.

It wasn't that Parras was a bad guy. He wasn't. The townspeople of Park Hills loved him. He was easy-going most of the time, helpful, and had pretty much kept serious crime off the streets of the small Ozarks' town. But the kidnapping of Tina changed the good sheriff's demeanor. It was the first kidnapping in Park Hills, and residents were fearful that it might happen again. Parras wanted nothing more than to find the deviants who took Tina. He was certain he would find them and sure as hell didn't need the FBI messing up his investigation.

From that day on, there was no cooperation between the local police and the FBI. Despite warnings from both Terry Moffitt and Booger, Parras continued his own investigation.

Parras was convinced the abductors were sickos who came down from St. Louis, which was a little more than an hour's drive away. The old broken-down station wagon spotted with Tina in the backseat was a solid clue and reinforced Parras' theory that the culprits were outsiders. No one he knew in Park Hills drove a car like that, and the car had not been spotted in town since the abduction.

There were few clues and even fewer witnesses. The bicycle lying on the ground in the exact spot the abduction took place; The rubber marks left on the street when the car sped away; The three young men spotted in the car; the description of the station wagon and witnesses spotting the car leaving town and taking Highway 67 North. Those were the clues, and none of them were particularly helpful in identifying the suspects.

T.J. and Chad were the best witnesses. They gave details of the car and details of the three suspects. "All were young," T.J. said. "Teenagers, maybe in their early twenties. Scroungy, wearing jeans and tee-shirts. The one that grabbed Tina had long hair and was thin. The other two were harder to see in the car. One was driving. The other was in the back seat."

He heard Tina scream. Saw her being dragged into the back seat of the station wagon. She looked his way one last time and screamed his name as the station wagon sped away.

Booger's first look at the crime scene told him a lot.

"I think at least one of the abductors is local," he said to Terry Moffitt. "The street where she was abducted is not a main road. The abductor knew about this area and knew the streets of Park Hills. I am certain of it. They've been here before. Most likely have lived here or are still living here."

"So, you don't think this was a random crime?" Moffitt asked.

"Well, I think it was a crime of opportunity. Those boys may have known Tina. In fact, I'd be willing to bet at least one of them knew her."

"Why's that?"

"She either came up to the car, or something they said got her attention because there wasn't a struggle prior to her being taken. The first scream her boyfriend heard was when she was already in the backseat of the station wagon. I think she probably knew one or more of the boys in that car. They most likely stopped to ask a question or talk to her, and she was taken off-guard when one or more of them jumped out of the car and grabbed her."

"What about the station wagon. Do you think whoever owns it lives in Park Hills?"

"No, I doubt we'll see that station wagon come into town again. Whoever owns it, most likely is from another area. Or, the car was stolen. Either way, we won't find that car around here."

"Well, then, it is unlikely that all three suspects are from Park Hills."

"You're right. I figure only one suspect lives or lived in town. If that person still lives here, the other two were likely visiting him. Maybe friends, maybe relatives."

"So, you think this was a crime of opportunity, and Tina was just in the wrong place at the wrong time?"

"Yes, basically. Those boys had a purpose for

driving around Park Hills at 10:30 at night. They were looking for a victim. Maybe a young girl, maybe not. But they had evil intentions, and Tina was alone late at night with few witnesses on the road. They must have seen T.J. and Chad. But their presence didn't stop the crime from happening. That means those abductors must have been highly motivated to carry out the crime to risk being seen by two boys less than a block from the abduction. Maybe they were on drugs. Probably, they had been drinking. They would have talked about the crime ahead of time. They would have discussed what type of victim they were looking for. They would have discussed what they were going to do with her. That means we're not dealing with one pervert but three perverts. Chances are, all three of these boys have done this before or something nearly as sick. And I'm guessing that this won't be the last time they do something like this."

"Serial killers?"

"Possibly. One thing is for certain. I doubt anyone with find Tina Mae Cooks alive."

CHAPTER 7
MOTHER'S DIARY

"I've never gotten over that case," Booger told Mason and Rose. "My role in the investigation was cut short. Tina Cooks was simply in the wrong place at the wrong time. She had left her brother's baseball game, grabbed an ice cream cone, and went home to get her bicycle to ride over to her boyfriend's house. It was after 10 pm, arguably too late for a thirteen-year-old girl to be out alone. But, then again, this was a small town in the 80s. People were trusting, and kids were more independent."

Sitting in the bar in north Springfield, Mason and Rose were now Booger's audience. It seemed the three of them were equally fascinated with the details of this thirty-year-old case.

"It was a warm summer evening. Few cars were on the road. She planned to visit her boyfriend for a few minutes before heading back home in time for her 11 pm curfew. She found her boyfriend, T.J., hanging out with his best friend outside his home. They talked for a few minutes before Tina began to ride her bike back home. The sound of a car driving slowly down the block could be heard directly behind her. Someone shouted at her. She turned to look. In an instant, she was dragged off the bike screaming and thrown in the back seat of the station wagon. 'T. J. help me,' she screamed as the station wagon drove away. There was nothing T.J. could do. It all happened in a matter of several seconds. He would describe the car later to police and tell them that there were three young men in the car, that the man in the passenger seat grabbed Tina and threw her in the back."

"Okay, now you're just repeating stuff," Rose said. "Did the police never find the killers? I assume Ben was one of the teens in the car, right?"

"Cops eventually figured out that a boy named Nathan Willamson was the main suspect," Mason said. "He admitted to her murder in jail but was already serving a life sentence for a pair of murders. The car belonged to him. It was believed that Ben Squires was one of the two boys involved – the other was a friend of Nathan's named Tim Robin, who was also serving a life sentence. Sherriff Parras decided not to take Nathan or Tim to trial after consulting with Tina's family. They were content that at least two of the instigators of Tina's murder would never see the light of day. Ben Squires was never seen again. His family had moved away, but it didn't matter. Ben was thought to be a minor character – a good boy caught in the wrong place at the wrong time."

"Yeah, I only recognize Ben's name from following the case in the newspapers," Booger said. "When I was involved, we were hunting for the car, and Parras and I couldn't agree where it might be found. I was certain these were local boys, and he just knew it was teens from the big city."

"And so, Parras got you kicked off the case?" Mason asked.

"Yes, that's right. Looking back, it must've been around that time the Squires' family left town."

"That's when they changed their names!" Mason said, louder than he meant to. Luckily, no one beyond their corner table noticed anything in the noisy bar. He continued with a softer tone: "They became the Collins family. Ben Squires became Wade Collins. And Wade Collins became Ben Sawyers. It's almost his original name!"

"I never knew where they went. It's making sense now, though. Wow. Ben Squires became your Wichita serial killer," Booger said.

"How interesting," Rose said.

"That's right. The details of their family life in Park Hills were recorded in Mrs. Squires' diary," Mason said. "Well, at least, most of them. There were pages missing – ripped from the diary. She must have said things that either she or Ben would remove."

"It is pretty incredible," Booger said, almost lost in thought.

"Yes, tell us more about the diary," Rose said to Mason.

"Sure. Well, Janie was vague. It was clear she suspected her son in the abduction of Tina Cooks, but I've always wondered how much she actually knew. As I said, some pages were missing. According to the diary that remained, she convinced her husband that their son was innocent and that the family needed to move away and change names. She was certain they needed to distance themselves from this investigation. They could start over in Wichita, where she had some family. The husband, an alcoholic, reluctantly agreed."

Mason paused before summing up. "Wichita was the perfect place to hide in retrospect because they were never found. And it seemed the Collins family lived a relatively normal life for about two years before the father, Ronald, began to drink even more heavily than he did in Park Hills. He always had a drinking problem, but the pressure of changing lives and the reality of what his son really was became too much for him. He resented his son. And when he'd get drunk, he'd beat him."

Now, Booger and Rose were just listening.

"Drinking became his way to deal with it all. He couldn't talk to his wife about their son's problems. She refused to believe that Wade had done anything wrong. She coddled her son. They become very close to each other, more best friends than mother and son. And Ronald's drinking spiraled out of control. One day, the arguments turned terribly violent. Janie was thrown against the wall of her bedroom. Wade decided to fight back against his father. That's when Janie murdered her husband. For months, the mother and son lived a peaceful, happy life. But Janie would eventually need more. She needed a man in her life, a husband, a lover."

"Yes, and Wade, or umm, Ben, would hunt them down. This is the stuff that turned him into a serial killer," Rose said.

"Yes," Mason said. "Months after her husband's

death, she began to go into bars, seedy bars, bars where men would prey on her. Usually, she dressed in short, red dresses with a low neckline that was particularly flattering to her large breasts. Wade didn't approve, but there was nothing he could do about it.

"A collection of one-night stands led to several bad relationships, mostly with married men. They used her. Janie fell in love several times, all in failed relationships. None of the men were willing to leave their wives. Each time a relationship fell apart, Wade was there to pick up the pieces. Their bond would strengthen for a while.

"Wade discovered the diary one night after a particularly rough break-up his mother had with a new suitor. He saw her writing in the diary. Getting a hold of his mother's most personal thoughts became an obsession with him. Whenever his mother was gone, he would read her diary."

Mason continued, fueled by the fact that someone was listening. He had someone to share this with. "Wade began to follow her when she went to bars. He watched from a dark corner as she picked up strange men. He followed them to hotels and apartments. He watched through windows. With every failed relationship, his mother would sink further into depression. He tried to make her happy. He took care of her, fixed her meals, sat with her at night, and talked about their future. Nothing seemed to work. One night, while he was at work, she hung herself. Wade found her when he arrived home. That was the lowest point of his life. He was completely alone. He took his mother's diary and read it over and over again. We found his fingerprints all over the book. They matched the cigarettes I'd find in the woods after we thought Wade had drowned. It was the only clues he'd left behind. His hatred for what she had become and for the men that treated her wrong must've become overwhelming."

"That's when he began to go to the seedy bars, watching and waiting for someone to remind him of his mother. Or of one of the bad guys she'd date," Rose said, noticing that Mason liked to talk as much as Booger.

"Yes," said Mason. "In what I believe is the first case, a woman in a red dress walked in, sat at the bar, and began a conversation with a strange man. From the conversation he overheard Wade knew she was married. So was the strange man. Wade watched and waited. When they left together, he followed them. They went to a motel and checked into room 109. The boy watched through the window as they got undressed, laid down together, and began to make love. When they had finished and dressed, the motel room door opened, and they began to walk out. Wade was waiting for them. He had taken a long steak knife from his mother's kitchen drawer. The man was first. He didn't even have time to scream before his neck was slashed. The woman's screams were largely silent. She was in shock. Her mouth moved, but nothing came out. Wade threw her on the bed, attacked her, and when he was finished, he cut her throat. That couple, I believe, were his first victims. The excitement he felt was overwhelming. The evil inside him had finally taken control."

He continued. "Three days later, he struck again. The more he killed, the more he refined his actions, developing a kill kit that he carried with him, striking late at night when there were no witnesses. Six victims over a three-week period. He wondered if and when someone would stop him. The police were slow to admit that they had a serial killer loose in Wichita. It was the same time that the BTK killer roamed the streets of Wichita. For a while, the police thought the two killers were one and the same. But their M.O. was totally different. They eventually moved me from the BTK cases to this one, the hunt for Wade Collins, although we had no idea who he was at the time. Wade became my obsession. I studied every crime scene, all married men and married women, all murdered late at night after leaving seedy bars. Most were killed in their cars or in motel rooms. Some of the women were raped. Some were not. All were killed with knives. At least that was how it was for the first six victims."

"So, there were more?" Rose asked.

"Yes. Then he began to change. The first daylight attack happened. A woman wearing a red dress left a grocery store and headed home. Wade was waiting in the parking lot. He followed her. When she pulled into her suburban driveway, he followed her inside the unlocked door. He raped and murdered her. A witness described his car driving slowly down the block. He was getting more brazen, more willing to take chances. It seemed he wanted to get caught. Or, at least, he didn't care if he did. That was his only attack in broad daylight.

From that point on, he found his victims in the daylight and followed them home. But then he would wait until the middle of the night before invading the home. Still, there were no clues left behind. It was about that time that I moved into a mobile home park on the south side of town," Mason said. "I was single and obsessed. I thought I could find him there or near there because three murders took place in the mobile home park. But he was always a step ahead. It was the murdered married couple that nearly broke the case wide open. That was how we found the diary. It was left at the murder scene. It turned out to belong to Wade's mother. It detailed several of the men who had affairs with Janie Collins. The murdered man turned out to be one of them. He had begun hunting men and women that did his mother wrong, which were outlined in the diary."

"It wasn't random anymore?" Booger asked.

"No. He was going after specific people now. It was about that time that I met Beverly. She lived in the mobile home park across from one of the victims. She also worked the graveyard shift at a local diner. I began visiting her there. We became good friends and eventually lovers. I didn't know it at the time, but it turned out that she was one of the women written about in the mother's diary. Beverly, an attractive blonde in her early thirties, had stolen one of the married men that Janie was having an affair with. It sent Janie into a tailspin of depression. And now, Wade was following her. There was a failed attempt on her life. I had arrived just in time to chase the murderer off. After that I took her to a small cabin in the woods I had near Darby. It was a peaceful place and somewhere that I thought I could protect her. But Wade discovered where we were and came for Beverly. I arrived just before he attacked her and chased him into the woods. At the foot of a large lake, I shot him. He fell into the lake. I thought he was dead, but after days of dragging the lake, no body was found."

"That's incredible," Rose said.

"Yes. I'd hoped he'd died but felt uneasy, you know. A week later, I discovered cigarette butts near an old tree about fifty feet from the cabin. I knew those cigarette butts were his. There was no mention of him smoking in the diary, but I just knew they had to be his. And then the fingerprints confirmed it. My chief wanted me to drop the whole thing. As far as he was concerned, Wade died in that lake, and cigarette butts proved nothing, and I couldn't argue. But, all these years, I've been waiting for Wade to reappear. Looking at cases in Missouri specifically where police thought they might have a serial killer on their hands. Nothing has ever looked like Wade. Until here and now."

"Whatever happened to Beverly?" Booger asked.

"She died a few months later in a car accident."

CHAPTER 8
SOMETHING ABOUT MARY

At a time when Ben Sawyers needed a fresh start and some direction in his life, he felt lucky to have met Mary Brown. At first, she felt lucky, too. She had been lonely and dreamed of having a husband and children. They wrote back and forth for several weeks before Mary asked him out on a date.

"If I would have held my breath waiting for you to ask me, I would have passed out blue," she told Ben a few months after that first date.

It wasn't that Ben was shy. He wasn't. But he had problems talking to women.

Mary was beautiful, a little heavy, but she had a beautiful face and long, dark hair. He was very attracted to her.

Their first date at Red Lobster led to a second and a third, and so on. Three months later, they decided to get married. Well, Mary decided they would marry. Ben never actually asked her. One day, they found themselves in a mall window shopping when a jewelry store caught Mary's eye. Inside, she made her way to engagement rings and picked out the one she wanted. It took Ben six years to pay off the cost of that ring.

Mary walked into the jewelry store single and

walked out engaged.

That was pretty much how their entire marriage went. Mary called the shots, and Ben did exactly as he was told. And it wasn't a problem for him. He needed that discipline. He welcomed it. This was what he wanted when he started looking for a partner. He wanted a woman who could keep him in line. And it worked for a time, anyway. He went nearly ten years without giving in to his dark side.

Naturally, there were times he came close to sliding, like when he was grocery shopping and spotted a young woman in a short, red dress with long, dark hair. He followed her throughout the store, watching, getting more excited every minute. When her cart was full, and she started for the checkout line, he abandoned his cart and left the store.

Ben got in his car and waited. When she got to her car, he watched her every move, walking down the parking lot aisle, opening her trunk, putting the groceries away, and finally getting in and driving away.

He followed her down the street. At a stoplight, he pulled up next to her to get a better look. He could see she wore a wedding band. In the back seat was a baby's car seat. She never looked in his direction, never knew he was watching her.

When the light turned green, he drove slowly to allow her to get in front of him. He pulled in behind her and continued to follow. At another light, she turned left. He continued to follow two cars behind her.

When she reached a subdivision, she turned in,

down one road, and onto another, turning three times before reaching a destination. When she pulled into her driveway, Ben was only a few houses away. He watched as the automatic garage door opened.

That's when he saw the other car parked in the garage. That was when his dark urge began to fade. Still, he parked the car and watched as she unloaded the trunk and went back into the house. He watched as the garage door slowly closed. Then he drove away.

That night, Mary was not happy when he returned home with only half of what he needed from the store. She screamed at him. "You stupid idiot! I sent you for one little errand, and you can't even do that right."

Life with Mary was not easy. She belittled Ben on a regular basis. He cowed to her every time. On the surface, he appeared to be weak, unable to stand up for himself. Inside, however, was the darkness. It was ever-present, slowly trying to surface and take control. Every time she would snap at him, his darkness got a little stronger.

Six years into their marriage, Mary's father spent a year in Ecuador as part of a mission trip. Her mother was alone, so Mary proposed she move into the city with her and Ben. He had never gotten along with Grace. She was a loud, obnoxious, and controlling woman, much like Mary. She never thought much of her daughter's husband either. He didn't have a good job. He didn't have much money, and she didn't respect him for it.

With Grace, just like Mary, Ben wouldn't stand up to her. He took her insults, ignored her laughter in his face, and the rude comments she made when she thought he couldn't hear.

After she moved into the house with Mary and Ben, the insults became even worse. Now, there were two women barking orders at him every day. Mary and her mother often joined forces in humiliating Ben. Life in the house became a sort of hell for him. Still, he didn't fight back. On the surface, his wife and mother-in-law were in total control. Underneath, however, the darkness was getting stronger.

One day, he'd had enough. He was working a minimum-wage job at a cardboard factory at the time, and one of his co-workers was sick. That meant, in effect, he had twice as much work to do and half the help. At the end of the day, when he came just short of meeting his production quota, his boss yelled at him, saying Ben was in jeopardy of losing his job.

When he came home that night, he was physically and emotionally exhausted. And that's when Grace started in. She could sense weakness in him, and she enjoyed belittling him when he was down. First, she said to Mary in clear earshot of Ben that it was a shame her husband didn't have a real job. She said he was an embarrassment. "He can't support you. He's no provider. One of my girlfriends asked the other day what your husband did for a living, and I said he was a professional bum."

This set Ben's teeth on edge. He tried to ignore her and went into the other room. He shook his head, fighting off the demons. Still, he could hear Grace.

Continuing on, "You should divorce that idiot,"

she said with a gleeful sneer. "He'll never amount to anything. If you leave him, maybe you can find a real man to take care of you."

It was too much. She had gone one statement too far. He told himself then and there that she'd pay. And she did.

That night, when Grace was sound asleep, Ben went into her bedroom. Quietly, he approached the bed. He pulled out the needle from his pants pocket. A shot between the toes would not leave any visible mark. When the needle went into her skin, she began to wake up. Ben injected the poison quickly. Then he grabbed a pillow and forced it over her face to muffle the sound of her screams. He didn't want to suffocate her. That was unnecessary and could be picked up by a medical examiner in an autopsy. Ben just wanted to keep her quiet. A minute later, she stopped fighting.

Mary was devasted at the loss of her mother. The coroner ruled the death to be from a massive heart attack. Grace was a large woman, over 300 pounds and nearly seventy years old, and all the signs pointed to a heart attack. No one suspected a thing. Well, almost no one.

When Mary's father returned from Ecuador for the funeral, he spent a lot of time with his daughter and Ben. They helped him make all the arrangements. He knew his wife was in poor health, and so he wasn't shocked that she'd had a heart attack. After the funeral, he had everyone come out to the farm for a meal made by the people from their church. It had been a heartwarming event for Allan. Everyone had been so kind in paying their respects. He knew his wife could be a bit much at times. She was very opinionated. Still, all who came told stories of times they'd had with her that made an impact. There was laughter and a lot of tears. After everyone left, he gave Mary a hug.

"Well, we got through it," he said.

"Yes, we did. You were great, Dad. Mom would have been proud."

At that time, Ben was cleaning up dishes and not paying attention. He was whistling Dixie without a care in the world. With Allan's head over his daughter's shoulder, still holding the embrace, he stared at his son-in-law for a moment. "Why is he so happy? He always hated her."

Allan never said anything to Mary or Ben, but he'd never forget that moment either.

For months after the funeral, Mary was sad and withdrawn. She stopped insulting Ben and went into a deep depression. He was there every step of the way to nurse her back to health. She became dependent on him much like his mother had after his father died. He fixed her food, put it on a tray, and delivered it to her bedroom just like he had done for his mother years earlier. Mary stayed in bed most of the time. For Ben, it was perfect. He had purpose and structure. He was loved and needed. Death, once again, had given him everything he ever longed for. Or it seemed to for a time.

For nearly a year, Ben nurtured his wife. He catered to her every need. Finally, with the help of medication, the fog of her depression lifted. It was a slow uphill climb for her, but she took the steps, and he took them with her. Unfortunately for Ben, when her health returned, so did the old Mary. The volatile, selfish, domineering, and demeaning Mary. And as her strength grew, his receded.

Before he knew it, he was her whipping boy again. And all the dark thoughts that had been held in check were surfacing just as they had before. He found himself missing work and following women.

The day Ben found the stray dog was one of the happiest in his life. He needed a friend, someone to talk to that wouldn't judge him. Murphy took over that role. She became completely dependent on him, and he became dependent on her, too.

Mary, on the other hand, despised the dog. She demanded Ben get rid of it or keep her in the yard. He chose to keep Murphy in the storage shed Ben built himself. And it was a good setup because the size of the shed allowed for Ben to spend time inside it with Murphy.

When he wasn't working or doing a chore for Mary, Ben hung out in the storage shed with his beloved dog. He even made it into a small workshop so he'd have an excuse to be there most of his free time.

Mary didn't seem to mind. Having her husband out of the house was a pleasant change for her. But the realization that Ben might care more for the dog than he did for his wife began to eat at her. Soon she demanded her husband spend more time in the house with her. The time he spent with Murphy decreased substantially.

That would change when Mary kicked Ben out

of the bedroom for the fifth time during their marriage. Being vanquished to a spare bedroom was a blessing for him. He waited until he was certain his wife was asleep, and then he quietly left the house and spent the night in the storage shed with Murphy. Ben even placed an inflatable bed inside and sneaked sheets and a comforter out of the house.

Murphy slept at the foot of the bed, curled up next to Ben's feet. For all his faults, the dog accepted him. He would do anything for that dog. For a little over five years, Ben and his dog were virtually inseparable. Ben viewed the dog as his key to sanity. The dog loved him and kept his demons at bay until the car accident. It took the fire department nearly an hour to pry Ben loose from the wreckage.

Mary would pay the ultimate price for having Ben's dog euthanized, but the ripple effects continued.

Shortly after Ben was released from the hospital, a man dressed in black broke a lock on the rear door of the Springfield dog pound. Inside, he unlocked the cages and set all the animals free. Then he poured gasoline on the floor and walls and struck a match. The entire place went up in flames in a matter of minutes.

The police knew it was arson, but they had no suspects as on-site cameras burned in the blaze.

Past midnight two days later, a man dressed only in black and wearing a mask broke a latch on a sliding glass door and entered a small ranch house. He used a flashlight to guide his way to the master bedroom, where he saw the man and woman sound asleep in bed, with no idea that an intruder had broken in. The man was on the right side of a king-size bed and had rolled over to the very edge. The stranger silently approached the man. Then took a needle out of his pocket.

When the man's wife woke up that morning, she discovered her husband was dead. Her husband was the veterinarian who euthanized animals at the animal center in Springfield.

A week later, another house was broken into just east of Republic. The man inside was also injected with a poison that made it look like he had a heart attack. He would also be discovered by his wife when she woke up the next morning.

That man happened to be the driver that ran the stop light.

The death certificates for both men read death from a heart attack. There was no autopsy performed on either man, which may have revealed the poison injected into their bloodstreams.

It was just too easy to rule the deaths as the result of natural causes. After all, this was Springfield. Murders just don't happen here very often, so why would anyone assume the worst?

Mary was dead, but Ben was never better. He was, in fact, full of life.

CHAPTER 9
THE DINER

Booger McClain had been a loner most of his life, and after his first wife passed away, he thought he'd never marry again. While he and Rose had been friends for over three decades, most of that time, they had lived very separate lives. Booger was independent. He had done his own thing his own way even after he hired Rose to help him.

That changed once he got married. They worked together on every case since the nuptials. Now, with this investigation, Mason Chase was part of the picture, too. He and Booger were becoming friends. They were working together like colleagues, much like Rose and he had done recently.

In a quiet moment in the car holding coffee, Rose recognized how she was feeling. She was jealous. She, too, had been a loner most of her life. She, too, had been independent. Her marriage, she thought, represented a new chapter in her life – one where she was part of a team of two. Now, she felt like a third wheel.

"Let me go with you on the stake-out," Rose said.

"Stake-out? Where'd you get that term, Rose?" Mason asked.

"I've always used it," she replied. "When you

follow someone, it's called a stake-out."

"We call it surveillance now."

"Well, whatever you want to call it, I want to come with you two on the stake-out."

"No, Rose," Booger said plainly. He was oblivious to how she was feeling. He wanted to keep his wife as safe as possible. "I need you to stay here, answer the phone, and keep an eye on the office. Mason and I can handle the surveillance of Collins."

The tone of his voice was not harsh but firm. This was a matter he didn't want to discuss further. Rose took in a breath, ready to respond, before holding it and then letting it go.

That night, Booger and Mason followed Ben Sawyers –and out of respect for Mason, they simply referred to as Wade Collins – from his work at the car dealership. It was the second night in a row they had tailed him. This time, they took Mason's silver Buick Regal to, as Mason put it, 'not broadcast to the whole world that Wade was being followed.' Booger had to admit his bright-red Corvette did seem to attract attention.

Wade left the lot at 8:10 pm and went to a Burger King three blocks away. From there, he drove north and then west of Missouri State University to a seedy part of town known for prostitutes and drugs. Just west of that area was a small bar called Terry's Tavern. Booger was familiar with the bar even before the three detectives followed the matches clue there and spent the night comparing stories. It was a small, dimly lit country music bar that catered to rough-and-tumble types – young and old alike. Its parking lot was populated by pickup trucks with oversized wheels and tires. On that first night, they never saw Wade come in. Now, Booger and Mason were following him inside, taking a seat at a table in a dark corner near the exit of the bar.

From where they sat, they could see him sitting at the bar, back turned to them.

"I'm Rachael. What can I get for you guys," a server on the downside of fifty said.

"Two Rye whiskeys on ice," Mason replied.

"We don't have Rye. Just whiskey," she replied.

"Okay, two double whiskies on the rocks."

A band in the far corner of the room was beginning to play. In front of the stage was a small dance floor.

The bar was beginning to fill up now. Some couples were there, but mostly, they were surrounded by single men and women. This wasn't the type of bar one brought a date, but it was the type where one found love, if only for a night.

"Damn, this whiskey has been watered down," Mason said after taking his first sip.

"Yeah, we should have asked for an unopened bottle," Booger responded.

Pretty soon, the venue was completely packed. It was a Friday night. The crowd was well-mixed, about half women and half men. Many dressed in country garb, but not all. A few women dressed like prostitutes, and they might have been, according to Booger. Some truckers. Some businessmen and women.

"It's a pick-up bar," Mason responded, letting

Booger know he had a good feel for the place. "People come here to get laid. The prostitutes work on the down low. It's mostly just regular people. Where I'm from, we'd call this a honky-tonk."

By 10 pm, the dance floor was packed. Couples began forming at tables and the bar. Still, Wade sat alone at the bar, moving only twice to go to the restroom.

At a little past midnight, a woman in a short, pink mini-dress with long blond hair took a seat next to Wade. They began talking.

"She's a prostitute," Booger said. "I've seen her leave the bar with two different guys and then reappear thirty minutes later.

The two detectives watched as Wade got up from his seat, took the woman's hand, and walked out of the bar.

"I'm going to follow him," Mason said. "I'm sure he's just going to the parking lot with her, but one of us should know where he is at all times."

"Sounds good," Booger said. "I'm just starting to enjoy this watered-down whiskey and loud country music."

Mason got up from his seat and exited the bar.

Booger motioned for the server to come over.

"Excuse me, hun. Here's $20. What do you say you bring us two doubles with ice of a bottle of whiskey that isn't watered-down?" Booger asked with a smile.

The server grinned back. "Yes, sir."

Booger watched as Rachael returned to the bar and whispered something to the bartender, who poured two drinks from an unopened bottle. Then Booger saw the bartender talk to a lightly dressed, heavily made-up woman at the bar, who turned to look at Booger.

A few seconds later, she got up from her seat and walked toward Booger's table. Rachael brought two drinks and walked away just as the woman in a leather mini-skirt got to the table.

"Want to dance cowboy?" she asked.

"No, thanks. I think my leg fell asleep," Booger responded with a smile.

"I bet I could wake it up," she said. "Mind if I sit down?"

He started to shake his head no before giving the matter an extra thought. "No, go right ahead. It couldn't hurt to talk."

"Buy me a drink?" she asked.

"Sure."

The woman motioned for Rachael.

"My name is Candy. What's yours?"

"Call me Fred," he said.

"Okay, Fred. You seem lonely since your friend left. I thought you might want some company."

"Well, that's nice of you, Candy. Do you come to this bar very often?"

"Most Friday and Saturday nights. It's a nice place to meet people."

"Yeah, I've noticed you've met several men already tonight."

"Oh, you've been watching me, haven't you, Fred?"

It was then that Rachael returned with a glass of champagne for Candy.

"That will be ten bucks," the server responded.

"Booger handed her twenty. "Keep it," he said.

"Thanks, mister," she responded.

"How'd she know to bring you champagne?" Booger asked when Rachael left the table.

"That's what I drink. She knows me," she said. "You know, Fred, if your leg is still asleep, I can rub it for you. I'm sure I can wake it up, and then maybe we can leave this place and get to know each other much better."

"How much?"

"What?"

"How much will it cost me to get you to rub my leg?"

"Twenty for a rub, $40 bucks for a tug, and $100 for the full treatment."

"My goodness, you are an enterprising young lady. I bet you know the regulars. Is it common to see three or four customers a night?"

"Sometimes more. I'm good at my job. Want to find out how good?"

Booger brushed past her question. "A few minutes ago, there was a guy sitting over there at the bar with a blonde."

"Yes. What about him?"

"You noticed him around? Ever rubbed his leg?"

"Yeah, I've seen him, but we don't talk. He always sees the same girl."

It was then that Mason returned to the table. "I see

you've been busy since I left," he said with a smile.

"Yeah, Candy, this is Tom. Tom, this is Candy."

"Candy, what a sweet name. If I've interrupted something, I can go away for a while."

"No, Candy was just leaving. I'm sorry, dear, but I'm happily married. But thanks for giving an old man a little excitement."

"Maybe your friend would like to party."

"No thanks, Candy. Maybe some other time."

"Well, you boys know where to find me if you change your minds," Candy said as she grabbed her champagne and walked back to the bar."

"My, my Booger McClain. What would Rose say?"

"Good thing we'll never know. Besides, nothing was going to happen. I wanted to see if she'd ever partied with Wade. She said he's always with the same girl."

"Interesting," Mason said, giving it an extra bit of thought. "He's in the restroom now. He'll be coming out soon."

"Where'd he go with the girl?"

"To his car. Twenty minutes then he came back in and went right to the restroom. Good thing I'm watching and not distracted."

"Yeah," Booger said with a nod of his glass.

About that time, their suspect exited the restroom and walked out of the bar. Booger and Mason got up from their table and followed him out.

The man at the bar got inside his car and drove away. Mason followed from a distance.

They followed him about two miles south and six

blocks east to a small restaurant called Shirley's Diner, not far from downtown. He parked the car and went inside. The place was nearly empty, with only two cars in the parking lot.

Mason parked across the street in a small used car lot, turned off his headlights, and watched. From that distance, peeping through the glass windows it was impossible to make out the faces of the people inside. "I wish I'd brought binoculars," Mason said.

"Me too," Booger responded.

There was a male customer at the counter, a man at a table, a server, and a cook. They watched as he took a seat at the counter.

The server came over with a cup of coffee and sat it in front of him. A few minutes later, she returned with a plate of food. He ate and had several more cups of coffee. It was nearly 4 am.

"He doesn't appear in any hurry to leave," Mason said.

The place was empty now except for the server and cook. A few minutes later, another cook and server showed up for the day shift. After talking to them for a few minutes, the cook and server, who had been there all night, left the diner with Ben, got his car, and drove away.

Booger followed. "What do you think is going on?" Mason asked.

"I don't know. Maybe they're friends."

The car went south several blocks, then west, and finally drove into an apartment complex. The car parked, and the three individuals went inside.

Thirty minutes later, Ben returned to his car and drove away. He drove directly back to his house and went inside.

Booger parked on the street about a half-block away and watched.

"Suppose he's done for the night?" Mason asked.

"I don't know, but I think we should wait until the sun comes up to call it a night."

A few minutes later, Ben emerged from his house in running shoes, shorts, and with a backpack on, and he began jogging down the road.

"I don't think we can follow him in the car while he runs. That'll be obvious," Mason said.

"No, but I think we can stay close enough to him to see where he goes," Booger replied.

The two detectives watched as he jogged down the neighborhood street and turned right. A few minutes later, Mason drove his Buick down the block and turned right in the same direction. They could see him in the distance. He followed, parking the car whenever he got within a 100-yards of Ben.

That worked well for about a mile when Ben began to take a series of turns. Soon, the two detectives had lost their suspect.

They returned to the house and parked the car down the block to await his return. Over an hour went by. The sun was coming up when Ben returned to the house. Nothing appeared out of the ordinary. When he went inside and shut the door, the two detectives left.

"Why don't you stay at our house?" Booger said to Mason. "We're going to be spending a lot of time together on this case and it just seems easier if you're staying with us. There's plenty of room."

"What about Rose? Will she mind?"

"No, Rose loves company."

Okay, then. It sounds good."

Booger pulled into the parking lot of the Drury Hotel. "Why don't you grab your clothes and checkout and I'll wait for you," Booger said.

Bags in the car, a few minutes later the two detectives headed back to Booger's office. It was nearly 7 am when Booger pulled into the parking lot of his office/home.

"Rose, we've got company," Booger shouted as he entered the house.

"I can see that. I'll make up the spare bedroom," Rose replied.

"Rose, I hope it's no trouble."

"Don't be silly. We have plenty of room, and you won't be any trouble at all."

"Thanks."

"How'd the surveillance go?"

"Good, I think," Booger responded. "We followed him to a seedy bar called Terry's. He spent most of the evening and early morning there, even picked up a bar lady of the night. Then he went to a small dirty spoon restaurant called Shirley's Diner. He stayed there for a couple of hours before driving the server and cook home and then going back to his house for the remainder of the night."

"And he wasn't out of your sight for any of the night?"

"Only when he went jogging."

"When was that?"

"Just about 5 am. I believe."

"That's interesting?"

"Why do I think you know something that we don't know, Rose?"

"Perhaps because I do. Your police scanner went off at 6:15 am. Seems that a young couple was attacked in their home on Adams Street."

"Shit," Booger replied. "That's less than a mile from Wade's house."

CHAPTER 10
THE BAR AND THE DINER

"We're going to that crime scene, Rose," Booger responded.

"Not without me, you're not," Rose replied.

"I need you here, Rose, to open the office and answer the phone."

"No, I'm coming, Booger McClain."

Booger took a moment and looked her straight in the eyes. It was an unspoken statement. "How serious are you?" She stared right back. "Fully serious." And then she softened her face. "This one matters." He knew when he was defeated. "Okay, but sit in the back," he said.

Rose didn't show it, but she was upset. She and Booger had done their investigating together since they got married. She knew in her heart she could spot things he couldn't see. She was part of the team. Now, she felt like a third wheel. Booger wasn't considering her feelings, and it bothered her.

Mason Chase had taken her spot. And not just figurately. He was riding shotgun in the Corvette to the scene. Booger wanted to take his car after not driving all night.

"Rose, I don't mind..." Mason said, but Rose

stopped him before he could finish.

"No, really. You should take the front seat. I'm smaller and can fit better in the back," Rose said.

"Are you sure? Well, thank you. I appreciate it," Mason said. She was right. He'd never fit back there.

"Rose doesn't mind at all, buddy. She's a sport," Booger said, laughing. "Tell me, do you follow Wichita State basketball?"

"I do," Mason said enthusiastically.

"How are they doing in that new conference? I've lost track of them since they don't play the Bears anymore."

Rose rolled her eyes.

A few minutes later, they were as close to the crime scene as they could get. The yellow tape prevented them from getting on the property. Neighbors had gathered outside.

"Mason, you and I should talk to the detective in charge. Rose, stay in the car," Booger said as they both rushed to action before Rose could grab her purse and sit up in the tight quarters of Booger's back seat.

"Hey, what the hell?" she said to herself with the doors closed and the men on their way.

Rose was not one to be told to stay in the car, and she had no intention of staying put. After climbing to the front of the two-door vehicle like a praying mantis navigating a tricky set of twigs, Rose composed herself, adjusted her hair, and let herself out with the last modicum of dignity she felt she had left. She decided immediately that if the boys were talking to the experts, she might have her luck with common folk and walked towards the crowd.

"What happened?" Rose asked a polite-looking lady in her 50s.

"Someone broke into the Givens' house and attacked Betty and Jim. We think they must be dead since an ambulance hasn't come to take them away," the lady with sharp silver hair said.

"Oh dear. So, it was a break-in?"

"Yes. Beverly saw it. Well, she heard it actually and then saw it," the lady said, looking straight at a young woman in her late twenties.

Taking a smooth step to her left like a seasoned reporter, Rose asked the young lady, "Oh my, what did you see, hun?" she asked in a motherly tone.

The young woman began to speak softly, her voice shaking. Her husband held her hand for support. "I was sleeping with the window open, trying to get some fresh air, when I heard the sound of glass breaking from next door. I looked out the window and saw a man with a ski mask on going through a window on the main floor of the Givens' house. That's when I woke my husband, and he called the police."

Rose let out a small gasp before opening her eyes wide and nodding, which let the woman know it was okay to continue.

"It seemed to take them forever to arrive, but it was probably just fifteen minutes. Just before they got there, the burglar came out the back door of the house and ran away."

"Was he wearing running clothes?"

"Umm, I don't know. It was too dark to tell. He just emerged from the house and ran out the backyard heading east."

"Have you told the police what you saw?"

"No, they talked to my husband briefly, but they still haven't asked me what happened."

"Well, yes, men sometimes just overlook us little women and think we don't know anything."

"Yes, that's right."

"Well, I'm going to help you, dear," Rose said before patting her on the back. She then whistled at a nearby officer with her fingers assisting as if she was trying to catch the attention of a passing vendor at a Cardinals' game. It was loud, and a bunch of people turned around. Rose was unfazed. The officer looked at Rose funny but then came over.

"Sir, this lovely young lady saw the intruder and had her husband call you guys. She has yet to give her statement. Can you make sure she talks to one of the detectives?"

"Umm, yes, of course," he said, taking the lady and her husband under the tape to a police vehicle where several other officers stood. Seeing that the woman was in good hands, Rose returned to the Corvette.

Rose sat in the backseat and watched her husband and Mason talk to Sergeant Willard Barnaby. Rose recognized the detective from pictures in the paper. He, evidently, was heading the investigation.

"Sergeant," Booger said, "we think you should

look at a young man by the name of Wade Collins. Well, Ben Sawyers is his current name. He went jogging early this morning, around 5 am, just six blocks from here. He didn't come back until after 6 am."

"You mean the salesman? Ben Sawyers? I've interviewed him already. He works at the Chevy dealership and sold two victims a car just days before they were murdered. He seemed rather quiet, maybe a little timid, not the type of person you would normally consider as a suspect in several murders. Did you follow him when he went jogging?"

"For a couple of blocks, and then we lost him," Mason responded.

"Oh, but you saw him enter the subdivision?"

"No. Errm, no."

"How about when he jogged back home? Were his clothes bloody?"

"Not that we could see," Booger said, now timidly.

"So, all you know for sure is that he went jogging for about an hour during the same time the crime took place?"

"Yeah, that's about it," Mason responded, "but what are the odds?"

"Well, pardon me, sirs, but you don't have squat."

"Just look at him, Sergeant. I'm telling you there is something off about him," Booger said.

"We've already looked at him. He's clean and has an alibi that he was working during two of the murders. If you boys are following him, I'm telling you that you're barking up the wrong tree. He's not the serial killer."

Booger looked at Mason and both were lost for words. A few minutes later, the pair were back in the red Corvette.

"Did you find anything interesting?" Rose asked.

"No, not really," her husband said. "The detective in charge wasn't going to talk about what he found inside. He thinks we are wasting our time watching Wade, too. They have ruled him out because of some bogus alibi. It's a huge mistake!"

"Uh huh," Mason agreed.

"So, you think Wade is the killer, but the police are off the trail?"

"Yes," they said in unison.

"So do I," Rose replied.

"Wait, what? So, you agree?" Booger asked. "Okay, Rose. What did you find out? I saw you talking to the neighbors."

"There was a witness, a young married lady that lives next door. She saw a man in a ski mask breaking into a window on the main floor of the house. He left out the back door and ran away."

"A jogger?"

"Maybe she couldn't see well enough in the dark. But he definitely ran away out the backyard and headed east."

"Wade's house is east of here, about six or seven blocks, I believe."

"Let's follow the roads back to his house, see how far it is, and if it is even possible for him to do the crime and get back home in an hour."

So, the three detectives got in Booger's car and drove to the suspect's house. It turned out to be less than a mile away. "He could have run to the house in ten minutes, run back home in another ten, and had nearly forty minutes in the victim's home. He had plenty of time," Mason concluded.

"But there would have to be blood on his clothes if he was the culprit," Rose said, not as a challenge but an observation.

"Culprit? Rose, you've been watching too much television. We call them suspects now," Mason said with a smile.

Rose was not amused. "Still, where was the blood?"

Booger and Mason looked at each other. Before either could answer her, she said, "I think we need to break into the house and check for bloodstained clothes."

"I like her!" Mason said to Booger.

"Woah, woah," Booger said, wanting to disagree, but about what he wasn't sure. "Let's just think about this."

"She's right, Booger."

A moment passed where Booger was clearly running through various scenarios in his head. Then, as if an idea had struck him, he said, "Gang, I think we're going to have to break into Wade's house."

"Yes!" Mason said.

"That's my idea, Booger!" his wife exclaimed.

So, they sat in the car and waited for Ben to leave his house. Nearly hours went by before he did. Booger and Mason were sound asleep in the car when he finally exited, jogged down the block, and out of sight. Lack of sleep from the night before finally caught up to the investigators.

After hours of doing next to nothing, Rose had to make a quick decision. "Should I wake them?" she wondered. For reasons she didn't fully understand, she decided against it. There was something inside her – a determination to prove her worthiness – that pushed her forward. She got out of the car, shut the door quietly so as not to wake up Mason or Booger, and she walked to the back of the house. There, Rose found an unlocked window and climbed inside.

The window was in the kitchen area. The place was a mess, with dirty plates in the sink and on the counter. It looked like no one had cleaned the kitchen in at least a week.

The living room was just as bad. Assorted papers, trash, and empty bottles. Rose noted one item that was missing: an ashtray. The psycho that struck Wichita was a chain smoker, according to Mason. Yet there were no ashtrays or packs of cigarettes anywhere.

In the bedroom, Rose found dirty clothes strung all around. She searched for any with blood stains, but she didn't find anything.

That was when she heard the front door open. Her heart skipped a beat. It was too late to get out of the house without being noticed, so she hid underneath the bed and waited. A few minutes later, Ben walked into the bedroom, took off his clothes, and went into the bathroom to shower.

That was when Rose climbed out from under the bed and walked out the front door.

When she arrived back at the car, both detectives were still asleep.

"Time to wake up, boys. It's time to go home."

"No," Booger said, yawning. "We need to get in Wade's house."

"Already done, boys," Rose replied. "Want to know what I found?"

"Yes," Booger replied. "But why didn't you wake us?"

"You boys were sound asleep, and I didn't have the heart to wake you."

"Okay, what happened?" Mason asked.

"Well, I didn't find any blood-stained clothes. I also didn't find an ashtray."

"A what?" Mason asked.

"An ashtray. If your suspect was a chain smoker like the psycho from Wichita, wouldn't you expect him to have ashtrays and cigarettes in the house?"

"Unless he gave up smoking," Mason replied. "Maybe he quit smoking."

"Yeah, that's a possibility, but if he hadn't given up smoking, wouldn't you expect an ashtray to be in the house?"

"Yes, I suppose so," Mason replied. "But, it makes just as much sense that he gave up smoking."

That night, after resting at the house, the trio decided to head to Terry's Tavern to see if they could find Ben there. Sure enough, at a little past 9 pm, he came in the front door. Rose, Booger, and Mason saw him enter as they were perched at a table in a dark corner of the bar.

"Can I get you something to drink?" A young, blond-haired server named Shirly asked the investigators shortly after their suspect arrived.

"A bottle of Rye whiskey unopened and two glasses with ice. Also, a bottle of white wine," Booger said, distracted.

"We don't have Rye Whiskey. Can I get you something else?"

"How about a bottle of Black Jack? Unopened."

"Yeah, we have that," Shirley said. "I'll be right back.

"Why the unopened bottles?" Rose asked.

"They water down their drinks here. A fresh, unopened bottle will ensure we get what we're paying for," Booger replied.

A few minutes later, Shirley returned with a bottle of Chardonnay and a bottle of Black Jack, both unopened.

"Do you want me to open the wine for you, ma'am?" Shirley asked.

"Yes, please," Rose said.

Booger poured his wife a glass of wine and then poured two glasses of whiskey, sat back, pulled out two cigars, handed one to Mason, put the other in his mouth, and lit it.

"Oh, a stake-out doesn't get any better than this," Booger replied taking a sip of whiskey and a drag of his stogie.

Just then, the band began to play country music.

"I was wrong," Booger replied. "It does get better!"

Ben was seated at the bar in what looked like the same chair he sat in the night before.

"What do you think of the cigar, Mason?"

"Best one I've had in a long time."

"Yeah, there's a little cigar shop in Springfield that special orders them for me. I'll take you by there sometime, and you can order some."

"Thanks."

"The whiskey isn't bad either."

"Yeah, if a place doesn't have rye, I'll settle for Black Jack, but it doesn't have quite the smooth finish of Rye."

"Let's dance, Booger. Mason can keep an eye on Wade."

"Yeah, you two go ahead. I'll be fine," Mason said.

"Okay, then, baby, let's show these youngsters how to two-step."

Booger and Rose hit the dance floor for two two-step songs and then a slow dance.

"Booger, do you still love me?" Rose said in a dramatic, half-joking voice.

"Yes, you know I do. You mean everything to me. What brought that on?"

"Of course, I know you do. I guess I've been feeling sorry for myself lately. You rarely say it anymore, and with Mason here, well, you two boys seem to have more fun when I'm not around."

"Oh, that's just not the case, sweetie. I've got to admit, it's nice to have a guy friend around, but that has nothing to do with us. Mason is an old detective like me. It's good to have someone like him help me with this case."

"But Booger, we've always worked alone before and have done perfectly fine solving cases."

"Yeah, but this is different. Mason knows the serial killer. He had run-ins with him in Wichita. He can really get in the mind of Wade?"

"But are you sure that Wade is the serial killer?"

"Yes. I'm confident he is."

"What about the lack of ashtrays?"

"I agree that's odd. But, it's like Mason said, Wade probably gave up smoking after he left Wichita. That was a long time ago."

"Maybe."

With the dancing done, Rose and Booger returned to the table to join Mason. Booger could tell his wife still wasn't satisfied with their conversation.

"What's wrong, honey? Don't you think Wade is the guy?"

"Yes. Well, maybe. It's just that he seems to be living such a normal life. I would expect a serial killer that has murdered over a dozen people would act a little strange."

"Sure, but it might be there's a side to him that we haven't seen before. Maybe he's got like a split personality – lives a normal life most of the time but then becomes a monster every so often."

"Doesn't it bother you that he went over ten years without showing the dark side of his personality? He was married for that long and never attacked anyone?"

Now, Mason chimed in. "Allegedly. Just because there is no proof that he attacked someone during that period doesn't mean he didn't."

With this, the group got quiet and returned to watching Ben at the bar.

At a little past 2 am, he got up from his barstool and left. The trio was quick to follow him. He got in his car and went to Shirley's Diner.

"This is the same diner we went to last night!" Booger said as Mason took a parking space across the street in an empty lot. He took out his binoculars and began to watch.

Ben took a booth near the rear of the diner. The server, a young, red-haired, thin woman in her mid-twenties, brought a cup of coffee and sat it down in front of him. They talked for a few minutes before she walked away. The server went back behind the counter and handed an order to the cook, who was clearly working over the grill. A few seconds later, he cracked three eggs and threw them on the grill.

When the food was finished, he plated it and handed the food to the server through the kitchen window. She delivered it to Ben and took a seat across from him. They talked and laughed for several minutes.

Booger described everything he saw to Rose and Mason.

"Gotta be a breakfast order," Booger said. "He was cracking eggs."

"Let me look for a while," Mason said.

Booger handed the binoculars over to Mason and sat back and relaxed.

"Got that thermos of coffee with you?" Booger asked Rose.

"Yeah, want a cup?"

"Yes."

The coffee had been sitting in that thermos for nearly eight hours. It was no longer hot and tasted like metal. However, it was strong, and that was all Booger cared about.

"Want a cup of coffee, Mason?" Rose asked.

"Sure, thanks."

Rose poured a second cup and handed it to him. Mason took a large gulp and knew instantly he'd made a mistake. He began gagging. "Geez, it's just a little too strong for me."

Booger smiled.

"Oh, I'm sorry, Mason," Rose said. "Booger likes his first cup of coffee to be extra strong. I figured with the stake-out, we'd need a strong coffee to help keep us awake."

Two customers left, and now Ben was the only one in the diner who wasn't working.

Mason watched as the cook came out from behind the grill, walked over to Ben's table, sat down, and began to talk.

"Damn, I wish that cook would turn around so I could get a good look at him," Mason replied.

The cook sat with his back to the front window. A minute or so later, the server came over and took a seat next to the cook.

Thirty minutes went by before another customer walked in. That was when the server and cook got up from Ben's table. That was when Mason got a good look at the cook for the first time.

He put down the binoculars and shouted, "Shit!"

Booger grabbed the binoculars and looked.

"Damn," he said.

"Wait, what?" Rose asked before she took them from her husband. Rose looked through them, but it was too late. The cook was back at his station now. His back was turned to Rose. "What did you boys see?"

"Can you see him?" Mason asked.

That's when the cook turned to look at the front door as another customer walked in. That's when Rose saw the cook's face for the first time.

"Twins," Booger said.

"Crap," she responded. "They look identical. Wade has a twin brother? Really?"

"Did you know he had a twin?" Booger asked Mason.

"No. I'm floored, honestly."

CHAPTER 11
THE TWIN

Just before 4 am, Ben Sawyers, walked out of the Shirley's with a server and his twin brother, a cook. They three got in Ben's car, and he drove away. Ben went to the same apartment building he went to the night before. All three got out of the dealer-plated, blue Ford Escape and went inside.

An hour went by before Ben emerged from the apartment building, got in his car, drove straight home, and went inside. Thirty minutes later, he came out of the apartment in his running clothes and took off jogging down the block.

Again, like the night before, Booger followed Ben until he lost sight of him about half a mile away. Like before, Ben returned an hour later. This time, however, there was no call for officers to respond to a crime in the area. The police scanner was silent. With Ben back at home and the adrenaline rush of discovering their suspect had an identical twin having run its course, the detectives retired for the night.

After Rose woke late that afternoon, she began researching the Squires family. For two days, while Booger and Mason continued their stake-out of "Wade Collins," she dug up everything she could on the family.

Janie Squires had given birth to twins in 1975.

"One was named Ben, and the other was Kyle, according to a birth announcement I found in the Farmington newspaper. That twin must be the cook at the diner," Rose said. "And her husband, Ronald, was briefly married before. I couldn't tell if he'd had any kids before the twins."

"Wow, that's a good find. I never knew anything about Kyle."

"Me either," said Mason. "Did Janie never write about him? Or are those what the missing pages in her diary are about?"

"I wonder if they gave him up for adoption immediately or if Wade, I mean Ben, and Kyle knew each other growing up," Booger said.

"Yeah, I wonder, too."

"One thing is for certain. Wade found his brother," Booger said.

Mason and Booger left the house soon after on a mission to get the name and as much information as possible on the cook at Shirley's Diner. It was nearly 5 pm when they pulled into the parking lot and went inside.

"Hi, ma'am. May we speak to the manager, please?" Booger asked.

"Well, I'm Shirley. I own this place. How can I help you?"

"My name's Booger McClain, and this is Mason Chase. We're private detectives working on a local case. You have a cook who works the graveyard shift. Is his name Kyle, by chance?"

"Yes, it is. What's this about?"

"Nothing really," Mason said. "We'd like to talk to him about his brother."

"Brother? I didn't know he had a brother."

"Yes, we just have a few questions for him."

"Well, he's not here right now."

"Look, that's fine. Any chance you have a phone number for him?"

"I'm not sure I should be giving that out. Are you with the Springfield police?"

"No, ma'am," Booger said. "Mason is with the Wichita police, and I'm a retired sheriff."

There was a moment of uncomfortable silence before Rose spoke up. "I'm a former waitress, myself," sensing that Shirley was skeptical of the men. She spoke with just a hint of a Southern accent. "These days, I try to keep my husband in line."

"Oh, really?" Shirley said, perking up. "Where did you work?"

"George's Steakhouse."

"George's! Get out. Did you know Kenny Teefertiller?"

"Like a brother."

"My sister married his cousin. Lord, that man could drink."

"It really was incredible. I saw him down a case one of Busch one Thanksgiving in the kitchen and he didn't even look drunk. I wonder how he is."

"Yeah, he died of the 'Rona."

"Oh no!"

The boys watched awkwardly, unsure of where this was going or just what they should be doing.

After a few moments of banter, Rose transitioned. "Look, we don't mean to trouble you. We really don't want to bother you if you can't share Kyle's contact information," she said before gently kicking her husband's shin out of sight to prevent him from objecting. "As the boys here said, we just have a couple of questions for him about his brother."

Now, looking the three of them over, Shirley smiled. "Well, no, I suppose it isn't trouble. Lemme grab his file."

A minute later, she returned with Kyle's address and phone number written on an order ticket.

"Thank you so much. We really appreciate it," Rose said with just a hint of a Southern accent. "The next time you see us in here, we're going to be customers."

"Well, that would be lovely."

"Thanks. Oh, and, if you don't mind," Rose said in what seemed to be an afterthought, "please do us a favor and don't tell Kyle that we were asking about him. We'd prefer to talk to him before he knows someone's looking to talk."

"Sure, of course."

With that, the trio left. Mason looked at Rose in a new light. "That was really remarkable, Rose!"

"Yeah, umm, good job, dear," Booger said reluctantly. "I mean, we could've eventually gotten that info, I'm sure."

"No, I don't think so. Rose, you really came

through," Mason said.

"Thank you, Mason," she said, looking straight at her husband.

Rose spent the next day researching Kyle Squires. She was able to discover that he'd lived in the Springfield area for most of his life. She found he was a graduate of Hillcrest High School and had racked up a significant criminal record – all drug offenses. His most recent charge was from five years ago for felony methamphetamine possession.

"It looks like he did a seventy-two-day stint in Chillicothe following his arrest for 16 grams. Is that a lot?" she asked Mason.

"Yes. Well, it's not a minor amount. I'm surprised he didn't do more time. I bet he turned on his supplier," he said.

"Yeah, the court record shows he pleaded guilty and was cooperating."

"Back in 2006, he had a charge for a minor misdemeanor possession of marijuana from El Dorado, Kansas."

"That's near Wichita!" Mason said with a crack in his voice. "My God, I just had a sickening thought. Is it possible that the real serial killer is Kyle Squires? Is it possible that I've been chasing the wrong person all these years?"

"No, don't think like that, Mason," Booger said. "Most likely, you've been chasing the right person. Wade Collins is most certainly the serial killer. You have his mother's diary, after all. You know what he went through as a child. You know he was in Wichita during the dates of the murders. Don't overthink this."

"Besides," Rose added, "he was arrested for a bar fight in Branson two months later. All indications are that he's lived in Springfield since at least high school. Plus, two of the murder victims bought a car from Wade just a few days before they were killed. That's not proof he committed the murder, but it puts him close to the victims. Another victim, only six blocks from his home, was murdered while Wade was out jogging. That certainly gave him the opportunity."

"Yeah, I'm sure you're right," Mason said. "This whole thing has thrown me for a loop."

"Mason, was there any DNA left at any of the crime scenes in Wichita?" Rose asked.

"Yes, from the first murder. We ran it through the state's criminal database but didn't get a hit."

"When was that?" Booger asked.

"2004," Mason said.

"So, Kyle wasn't in the state system yet?"

"Yes, that's right. You know, Wade always had a clean record. That's why we assumed there was never a match in the database. But if he has an identical twin, that changes things. In most instances, identical twins share the same DNA signatures. The same fingerprints."

"So, you could run things through the database again and maybe get a hit?" Booger asked.

"Well, with fingerprints, yes. But we never found any unexpected fingerprints at any of the scenes. All we had was what was on the diary and the cigarettes in the woods. Everything else was technically circumstantial. It just happened to be enough to convince the chief."

"Oh, I get it. So, if we could get a hair for either Wade or Kyle, you could see if it matches the book or cigarettes?" Rose asked.

"Yes, that's right."

"Well then, all we have to do is get a sample of one of the twin's DNA," Rose said plainly.

It was a simple but important statement. Booger and Mason both realized at once that they didn't have to prove Wade committed the murders in Springfield before connecting them to the ones in Wichita.

"Rose, you're right. We just need a hair or saliva sample to break the case wide open. But we should try to get both twins, just to be sure," Mason said.

"How do we do that?" she asked.

"We'll follow them until they discard something with their DNA on it, like food or a drink or a cigarette," Booger said.

The next morning, the surveillance began on both suspects. Rose took the day shift, staking out the apartment where Kyle Squires lived. Booger took the night shift.

Mason was assigned Wade, and he followed him wherever he went. They decided they'd try to get a sample from each of them if they could. Kyle was more difficult.

For the detectives' mission, Wade was fairly easy. Booger paid the bartender $20 for the unwashed mug he'd been drinking out of at Terry's Tavern.

Kyle was more difficult. He rarely left the apartment except to go to work or come back home. The woman he was living with ran most of the errands to the grocery store and other places.

For nearly a week, Mason or Booger followed him everywhere he went. One evening, they noticed that Kyle went on a smoke break behind the diner. Mason took a position close to him so he could watch him smoke. When he threw the cigarette butt down, Mason waited patiently until he went back inside; then, he grabbed the cigarette butt and put it in a plastic bag.

The trio of detectives had their DNA samples. Now, Mason just needed to convince the Wichita Police Department to run them. That proved more difficult than Mason thought it would.

The WPD was concerned that the DNA, taken without permission and by two people outside of the Wichita Police Department, would not stand up in court if the suspect went to trial.

"Just run the damn DNA. If it comes back as a match and we know who the serial killer is, then we'll get the evidence needed to bring them to trial, even if that means the DNA we took from them will be inadmissible in court," Mason was heard saying over the phone.

Finally, the WPD gave approval to run the tests. That was just the first step, though. Now, the sample waited. DNA testing was weeks behind. It could be a while before the WPD had an answer to whether the DNA matched that left on some of the victims.

In the meantime, the trio continued following both

suspects.

Booger and Mason did the surveillance while Rose stayed back at the office. Mason watched Kyle while Booger watched Ben.

Booger's watch landed him in Terry's Tavern most nights. That's where Ben spent most evenings. Same routine, drinking at the bar. Most nights Cristine showed up always wearing a red dress. They would have a few drinks together and then leave the bar together for a rendezvous in the black Cadillac.

Christine Coleman was a perplexing mystery for Booger.

"She's wealthy as all get out. She owns the car dealership. What does she want from him?" he asked Rose.

"Maybe she wants a young thang," Rose said, laughing.

"Hmm. And what about the red dress? Isn't it unusual to always wear the red dress?"

"Yeah, I can't help but think Wade has asked her to," Mason said. "Maybe it's part of his fantasy, or maybe she just likes the attention she gets wearing it."

Between 2 am and 2:30 am nearly every night, Ben left the bar and drove to Shirley's Diner, where he sat at a table near the back of the diner.

The parking lot across from the diner was where Mason and Booger met up to compare notes on the evening.

"Anything interesting happen tonight, Mason?"

"Yes, as a matter of fact. Kyle and his girlfriend

have a car that is parked at the apartment complex. Kyle left in it today and drove to the grocery store. He just sat in the parking lot for nearly an hour, then went inside the store, shopped for a few minutes, and came out with a bag of groceries, got in his car, and left. He went straight home."

"What kind of a car was it?"

"A red Honda Civic, older model with several dents in the front bumper area."

"A similar car was spotted following one of the victims," Booger said.

"We need to tail Kyle," Mason said.

"I think we need to tail both of them," Booger added. "Mason, you stick with Kyle, and I'll take Wade."

"Hey, what about me?" Rose said.

"Sweetie, you stay here and answer the phones. If we need you, we'll call."

Rose wasn't happy with that answer. He was lapsing into treating her like a secretary, and she didn't like it.

Since most of the victims had been attacked in the evening and early morning hours, the surveillance went from 7 pm - 7 am. Booger sat out in his car at Ben's house on the northside while Mason watched Kyle's apartment in center-city. Most of their time was spent sitting and waiting.

For Booger, he was used to the waiting. In all his years as a private detective, he had done surveillance many times, and most were the same, hours and hours of sitting and doing nothing. Waiting for one action that would seal the perpetrator's fate. In his experience, that action always came. Patience was everything in his line of work.

At a little before 11 pm, Ben left his house, got in a gray Chevy, a loner from the car dealership where he worked, and left. He drove straight to Terry's Tavern, parked in the back of the lot, and walked inside. Booger followed and took a seat in a dark corner of the bar.

"What can I get you?" a server by the name of Ann asked.

"Coffee and a shot of whiskey," Booger replied.

Ben took a seat at the bar and ordered a draft beer.

A country band was playing in the corner of the bar. The dance floor was crowded, and the place was nearly packed.

It was unusually late for the salesman to arrive at the bar. The previous times Booger had followed him there, he arrived about two hours earlier.

Sitting at the end of the bar and getting quite a bit of attention from male customers was a lady dressed in a bright red dress, short in length, that showed off her long, thin legs.

Booger watched as Ben walked over to her.

"Would you like to dance?" he asked.

"Sure," she responded.

Booger noticed Ben took the lady's hand and walked her toward the dance floor. The detective couldn't get a good look at Ben's dance partner. "Buzzin" by Amanda Kate was playing, and the couple began to two-step around the dance floor.

That was when Booger got a good look at the lady in red.

"Shit," he responded. Their suspected serial killer was dancing with Rose.

Booger was upset. He had told Rose to stay at the office and answer the phone. Granted, it was hours after closing time, but still, he didn't want Rose involved in the investigation. It was simply too dangerous for her, and Booger wanted to protect his wife.

"Can I get you another coffee and whiskey?" the server said.

"Just the whiskey and give me an unopened bottle along with a glass with ice in it," Booger responded. The house whiskey was watered down. He could barely taste it in his coffee. Ordering an unopened bottle was the only way to insure they didn't water it down.

"Yes, sir."

"Call me Booger."

"Okay, Booger."

The former sheriff watched as the song ended and Rose returned to the bar with Ben taking a seat next to her. He watched as the two talked and laughed. He watched as Ben took a hand and put it on her leg. A couple of minutes later, the server, Ann, arrived with an unopened bottle of Old Crown whiskey and a glass full of ice.

"Thanks," Booger responded, handing Ann two fresh twenty-dollar bills. "Keep the change," he responded.

"Thanks, Booger," Ann said with a smile.

He opened the bottle and poured a stiff drink.

Then, took a long swallow. Old Crown wasn't bad house whiskey. It wasn't as smooth as the rye whiskey Booger normally drank, but it wasn't bad, in his opinion.

Booger took another large swallow and reached for a stogie in his pocket before realizing smoking wasn't allowed in the bar. He fiddled with the brim of his hat nervously, helplessly, as his wife sat and talked to a man who liked to murder women in red dresses.

Fifteen minutes later, Christine Coleman entered the bar also wearing a bright red dress. Booger watched intently to see how she would react to seeing Rose sitting with Ben.

There was a short conversation between the two of them, and then Rose got up from her chair and walked toward the front door. Booger got up from his chair and grabbed her arm just as she was about to leave. "Mind if I buy you a drink?" he asked, pulling her arm toward his table.

"I was leaving, but I guess one quick drink wouldn't hurt," she responded.

Booger led her to his table.

"Ann," Booger hollered, seeing the server at the next table. "Bring me another glass with ice when you have a chance."

With Rose seated at the table, Booger asked, "Okay, tell me what you are trying to do, Rose."

"Well, I figured I would help."

"Why the red dress? You know you stand out in this place."

"Yeah, that's the idea. I know Wade is attracted

to women wearing red dresses, so I figured that was the best way to get his attention."

"Yeah, his attention and fifty other guys' attention."

"Why, Booger, you sound jealous."

"No, I'm just worried about you. How did you plan to protect yourself if something did happen?"

Rose opened her purse and pulled out a 45-caliber pistol. "With this, if I had to, but I didn't think that would be necessary. I knew you were following Wade, so I figured you would step in if anything happened. Plus, I wore extra make-up and did my hair different so he wouldn't notice me from the dealership. And I really think it worked. He didn't seem to remember me at all."

"Still, it is a dangerous game you're playing. I want you to go home and stay there."

"Booger T. McClain, I'm a private detective, too, and I can take care of myself. You need my help to determine who the serial killer is, but you're too stubborn to admit it. The red dress is the bait, and unless you want to shave your legs and wear it, I'm the person you need to draw the serial killer out."

"Okay, okay. I'll admit I need you, but no more going out on your own. Let's work together to catch this psycho."

"Sounds like a plan."

"Good, now go home and stay there tonight. We'll work on a plan tomorrow. But first, what did he talk to you about at the bar?"

"Small talk mainly. He did say that he would be back tomorrow night and hoped we could talk and have a drink together."

"Good, we'll plan on that."

"Now, go home and call me when you get there so I know you are safe."

"I will."

CHAPTER 12
LATE NIGHTS

After Rose left, Booger waited and watched. Christine and Ben appeared deep in conversation for nearly thirty minutes. Then, he got up and led Christine out of the bar and to her car for the next twenty minutes. Afterward, he came back into the bar while Christine started her engine and drove away.

Booger couldn't help but wonder what was going on between the two of them. "Were they just lovers, or were they more than that? Were they in love? Or was this just a series of one-night stands?"

Shortly after Christine left, Ben got in his car and drove to Shirley's diner. It was the same routine as previous nights. "When does this guy sleep?"

Booger had noticed that Ben typically went to work around noon and stayed until eight. Some days, he'd work 10 am to 6 pm. But most days, he wasn't sleeping until after his morning run. "How does he do it?"

Ben took a seat at a booth at the back of the restaurant. Kyle's girlfriend, the server, brought him coffee and a meal. When the crowd slowed, Kyle walked over and sat down next to his twin, and they talked for several minutes. Then, at a little past 4 am, the new crew arrived, and all three left in Ben's car to go back to the apartment complex.

This was also puzzling to Booger. "Kyle has a car. He parked it in the lot at the apartment complex. Why didn't he drive it to work? Why was it necessary for Wade to bring Kyle and his girlfriend home after their shift at the diner ended?"

Later that morning, the trio of detectives met in Booger's office to discuss what happened the night before and what their plans were for the next day.

"I made some fresh prune muffins if anyone wants one," Rose said.

"Thanks, Rose," Mason said, taking a muffin.

"Thanks, sweetie," Booger said, grabbing a muffin.

Booger looked in amazement as Mason gobbled down the muffin without any reaction whatsoever. "Had his wife's baking skills suddenly improved?" Booger wondered.

The answer came to him with the first bite he took. "No." The muffin was terrible, yet Mason ate the whole thing without complaining. Then he took a second muffin.

"These are fantastic, Rose," Mason replied, licking his lips.

All Booger could do was stare at him, wondering what was wrong with his friend. After cups of coffee, all three sat down in Booger's office to talk and strategize. It felt to him like things were going nowhere.

Booger took out two stogies from his shirt pocket, handed one to Mason, and put the other in his mouth. He struck a match and lighted both cigars. Then sat back in his recliner and took a long, deep drag of the cigar.

"Okay, Mason, what did you find out about Kyle?"

"He and his girlfriend left the apartment at 7:30 pm. They took a bus to the diner and began their shift at 8 pm. The diner was fairly busy, and there was nothing unusual that happened until midnight. That's when Kyle left the diner for the first time. He went out back. I got out of my car and went around to the rear of an adjacent building to see what was going on. I saw him meet with a young man – maybe in his early twenties. Kyle took money from the young man and handed him a small plastic bag. Then the young man left, and Kyle went back in the diner. This happened three more times before Wade arrived a little after 2 am."

"Drugs?" Booger asked.

"I don't know, but that's what it looked like, of course," Mason replied.

"We need to find out what's in those bags."

"Okay, do you want to tell Mason what you learned from your trip to the bar last night?" Booger asked his wife.

"As you know, I went to Terry's wearing a red dress, hoping to draw out Wade. He did approach me and asked me to dance. Afterward, we talked for several minutes. He was flirting with me just before Christine Coleman arrived and got upset that he was talking to me. Just before they left together to go out to the parking lot, Wade told me he'd be back tonight and hoped he would see me again."

"Woah, how come I didn't know Rose was going

to make a move on Wade?" Mason asked Booger.

"I didn't know. She did it on her own."

"Well, personally, I think it is too dangerous to involve Rose in this."

"Try telling her that."

"Listen," Rose began with an angry look, "I'm a detective now, too. I can take care of myself. Besides, Booger was in the bar. He would have stepped in if there was a problem. From what I can see, our suspect likes women wearing red dresses, and I doubt seriously if either of you two would look good in a red dress. If we want to catch Wade in the act, I'm the best bait you have."

"So where do we go from here?" Mason asked.

"We need drugs, I suppose," Booger said. "Assuming, of course, that's what's going on at the back of Shirley's Diner. Mason, I think you should get one of those bags of goodies that Kyle is handing out, but first, I want you to come to Terry's with me tonight. We need to keep an eye on Rose. If she does manage to get Wade to act on his urges, I would feel better if both of us were there to protect her."

"Yeah, no problem," Mason replied.

That evening, Mason and Booger arrived at the bar around 9 pm. They took a table in the back near the only exit and waited. Ben arrived at a little past 10, and Rose followed not long after. She was wearing another red dress. Rose took a seat next to him at the bar.

As an extra bit of precaution, Booger placed a microphone on Rose so that he could hear any conversation that took place.

"Is your girlfriend coming tonight?" Rose asked.

"Yes, but it will be around 1 am, so we have plenty of time to get to know each other."

"So, what do you want to know about me?"

"Are you a cop?"

"What? Why would you ask that? Of course, I'm not a cop."

"Sorry, but I had to ask. Up until last night, I've never seen you in here and you come in wearing a red dress both times. Red happens to be my favorite color, and if you're going to grab my attention, wearing red will do it."

"Red is my favorite color, too. That's why I wear it. As for not being in this bar before, you are right. Last night was my first night here. I just moved to Springfield recently and discovered this bar last night," Rose said, grabbing a cigarette out of her purse. Ben responded with a light. "Let me ask you a question."

"Go ahead."

"Is there a reason that you're worried about me being a cop?"

"No, not really. I'm not in any trouble if that's what you mean. However, there are working girls that frequent this bar and from time to time, and an undercover policewoman has been known to play that role to catch unsuspecting johns."

"So, you think I'm an undercover cop pretending to be a prostitute?"

"No, not necessarily."

"What do you think of me?"

"I think you're a very attractive woman that I'd like to get to know much better."

"And I think you're a player that has used that same line many times before. Let me set the record straight for you. I'm a married woman who came here for a few drinks, laughs, and to dance. I'm not looking for anything more, and if you think you're going to get lucky with me, you're wrong. I like you. But that's it, nothing more."

"I understand. Would you like to dance?"

"Absolutely."

Booger sat back in his chair and took a long, slow swallow of Old Crow.

"Well, she certainly set him straight," Mason replied.

"Yes, Rose is a tough lady. She won't take any crap off anyone. I'm just hoping she didn't scare him off."

"Not a chance. She did everything right."

At a little past midnight, Christine walked into the bar.

"I didn't think I'd see you again," she said to Rose when she saw her sitting next to Ben.

"No problem. I'm just here for a few dances and laughs, nothing more."

"Good, because I plan on wearing this boy out tonight, and I doubt there'd be anything left for you."

Rose laughed. Then she got up and moved to another side of the bar.

A few minutes later, Ben and Christine got up and walked outside.

Booger walked up to the bar, to where Rose was sitting and took her hand.

"Can I have this dance?" he asked.

"Yes, of course."

A minute later, they were slow dancing on the dance floor.

"You're shaking, Rose," he said.

"I'm sorry. There is just something about that guy that frightens me."

"Don't worry. You did fine, and Mason and I are here to protect you."

"He's a psychopath. I know he is. There is a darkness in his eyes, a coldness to him. He wanted to kill me. I could tell."

"Don't worry, Rose. I won't let anything happen to you," Booger said. "But seriously, why don't you take off and go back home. Mason and I will keep an eye on Wade for the remainder of the night. You'll be safe, and we can talk when I get back in the morning."

"Sounds good. I think I will," she said, with a deep sigh.

After the slow dance, Rose grabbed her purse and left the bar. In the parking lot, she encountered Ben. "That was quick," she said. "I figured you'd be gone for a while."

"So, you decided to leave rather than wait for me?"

"My husband's waiting for me. I need to get home."

"You know, I can't shake the feeling you look familiar. Like we've met somewhere before. How about one more drink?"

"No, afraid not. I need to leave."

"Okay, then. See you next time."

"Okay."

Rose continued to her car, got in, and left. Five minutes later, she noticed a car that appeared to be following her. She kept an eye on it for several blocks, turning several times along the way. The stranger continued to follow her. That's when she called Booger.

"Booger, there is someone following me."

"Oh shit. Can you describe the car?"

"No, it's dark, and the car is dark. I can't tell."

"Can you see the driver?"

"No."

"Booger, I'm worried. I had an encounter with Wade in the parking lot. He seemed weird. I'm worried he might be remembering me from the car lot."

"Dammit! You mean he's not with Christine?"

"No, she left. Is he in the bar?"

"No, he hasn't come back in."

"Shit. What do you want me to do?"

"Don't go home. Go to George's Steakhouse. I'll meet you as soon as I can get there. If he follows you into the parking lot, go inside. He wouldn't dare do anything with people around."

Booger and Mason left the bar right away to head to George's.

Rose did exactly as Booger told her. The drive to the restaurant was about ten minutes. When she pulled into the parking lot, the car that was following her pulled in, too. She jumped out of her car and ran inside.

Safely inside, she took a seat in the most crowded part of the restaurant.

"Coffee, please," she told the server.

Rose's eyes never turned from the front door. A few minutes later, a stranger walked into the restaurant, looked around and when he spotted Rose, he walked to her table.

"Ma'am, my name is Allan. I believe you are in danger."

CHAPTER 13
ALLAN

"I'm sorry, I don't believe I know you."

I'm Mary's father. Mary was married to Ben Sawyers. She disappeared a little over a year ago. I think he murdered her. He might have also murdered my wife, but I'm not sure. Anyway, I believe you are in danger. Do you mind if I sit down?"

Rose sighed deeply. "Ben Sawyers."

"What?"

"His name is Ben Sawyers. It used to be Wade Collins. Well, actually, it used to be Ben Squires. Maybe you should sit down."

"Yes, that would be great."

"So, tell me, Allan, why do you think my life is in danger?"

"Because you've got his attention now. I saw you flirting with him at the bar. I can see the way he looks at you, and I don't think you realize you're playing with fire."

"I get it. So you were following me?"

"No, well, yes. I was following him at first, but I couldn't help but notice the way he looked at you. When you left, I just knew I had to try to talk to you."

"So, what do you know about Ben? I mean, umm,

Wade. We've been calling him Wade, but he is actually Ben."

"Well, ma'am, Ben is a psychopath. I have given him the benefit of the doubt in the past, but those days are over. He is incapable of love. He's pure evil."

At just that moment, Booger and Mason walked into the restaurant, spotted Rose in the corner, and hurried over.

"Everything okay?" Booger asked Rose, staring at her booth-mate.

"Yes, dear. This is Allan. He's the father of Mary, who was married to Wade. Well, Ben. He knows him as Ben Sawyers. Can we call him Ben now? Anyhow, Allan came here to warn me that my life was in danger."

"Allan, this is Booger. He's my husband. And this is Mason. He's a detective from Wichita."

"Glad to meet you both. Gee, maybe you didn't need me looking out for you after all," Allan said. "But I'm a little confused. Did you say Booger is your husband?"

"Yes, that's right."

"Maybe I should explain," Booger said, taking a seat next to his wife. "I'm a private detective from Springfield. My friend, Mason, is a detective from Wichita. We are both watching Ben and believe he or his twin brother may be a serial killer who struck Wichita about twelve years ago and is now murdering people in Springfield. We've been watching him for several days. My wife Rose is the bait. We know Ben has a weird attraction to women wearing red dresses, so my wife dressed in one in hopes of getting him to act."

"Did you say twin brother?"

"Yes, Ben has a twin brother who works at Shirley's Diner. We've been keeping an eye on both of them. Even got DNA from them without their knowledge. We're hoping that when the results come back, we'll know which one is the murderer."

"Well, regardless of which one is the serial killer, I'm certain Ben killed my wife and daughter."

"Can I get you folks anything to eat?" a thin, brown-haired server asked.

"Just coffee, please," Booger responded.

The server grabbed a pot and filled up three cups of coffee. Can I warm your's up," she said, looking at Rose.

"Yes, please."

After the server left, Booger looked at Allan and asked, "Have you been following Ben for long?"

"No, only for a week or so. I got tired of feeling helpless. I don't really know how to be a detective or anything, but I thought maybe I could catch him somehow. Catch him doing something wrong. My wife died first. Heart attack. Or at least that's the official reason. Ben seemed all too pleased she was gone, so I thought it was fishy because they did not get along, but my wife was in bad health. Then, a couple of months back, my daughter went missing. Supposedly, Ben was in the hospital when she left him. He said he thought she went back to the family farm. I filed a missing-persons report with the police, but without evidence of foul play, there was nothing they could do. I've never had a good feeling about this guy. He's one of those quiet types, and those are the ones you have to worry about, you know?"

"Yeah, that's true," Rose said.

"There's been a couple of murders here recently that have reminded me of what happened in Wichita, so I took some time off work and came here to investigate this. I connected with Booger, and the three of us have been following him, too," Mason said. "I'm certain Wade, I mean Ben, is the serial killer there, but those murders stopped nearly twelve years ago. It's like he fell off the face of the Earth, but now he's back. Except he's Ben Sawyers now."

"Interesting. Well, I think it was around that time he and Mary got together," Allan said.

"Oh, really," Rose said.

"So, have you been hanging out at Terry's Tavern like us?" Booger asked.

"Yes. For a week, I've watched him in Terry's. I watched as an older woman walked into the bar night after night wearing a red dress, then leaving the bar with Ben and going to her black Cadillac with him for, what I think is a quickie. Afterwards, he comes back to the bar for a few minutes and then leaves to go to Shirley's Diner, the same routine every night until your wife got involved two days ago. I was worried that she might be in real danger because I know he's a psychopath. That's why I followed her here to warn her."

"Well, you're welcome to join us in the surveillance of the twins if you want. We can cover more ground with another person."

"Sounds good. I just want to see Ben get what's coming to him."

"Okay, great. Where are you staying?"

"The Drury Inn."

"No sense in doing that," Booger replied. "We've got plenty of room at our house. You can stay with Rose and me and Mason. That way, we can compare notes every day."

That evening, Allan moved into Booger and Rose's house. Rose made a cot for him in the living room. Around 9 pm, Mason watched the apartment complex where Kyle and his girlfriend lived. Allan watched the home of Ben. Booger would tail Rose as she went to Terry's. He took a seat in the back corner with good visibility to the bar. Allan would follow Ben to the bar a little later and take a separate table near the exit.

Rose took a seat at the bar and flirted with Ben. But that's as far as it would go. Every attempt Ben made to get Rose to leave the bar with him was unsuccessful. Rose danced with him but left the bar alone at 1 am. Booger followed her home to make sure she arrived safely. Allan stayed in the bar and kept an eye on Ben. When Ben left at a little past 2 am, Allan followed him to Shirley's Diner.

Mason was already there keeping an eye on Kyle when Allan arrived.

The routine was identical to previous days. Ben took a booth near the back. When business slowed down, Kyle sat with his brother and talked. Mason used binoculars to try to see what was going on between the two brothers. That was when he saw the money exchange hands between the two of them.

"Anything unusual go on tonight?" Booger would ask in the morning.

Mason explained about the money he saw change hands. "It must have been several hundred dollars," Mason said.

"Drug sales?" Booger asked.

"I think so. Kyle made several trips out back where he met with different individuals, exchanging a plastic bag of white powder for cash. It has to be drugs."

"So, the two brothers have an enterprising drug business?"

"It appears so. Kyle gives the drugs to their runners at night behind the diner and takes their money from the sales earlier that evening. Kyle and Ben divide the profits in the diner when no one else is around. At least, that's what I think is going on," Mason said.

"Where are they getting the drugs?" Booger asked.

"I don't know, but I think tomorrow night, we need to get into Ben's home and take a look."

That became their plan for the next night. Allan would keep an eye on Ben while Booger and Mason broke into his house.

That was the plan anyway, but plans have a way of changing. Allan kept thinking about Mason's conversation about the possibility of drugs changing hands at the rear of the diner. Part of him wanted to prove to the two detectives that he could be of use to them, and part of him wanted to get the evidence that Kyle and Ben were involved in drug distribution so he could alert the

Springfield police, who might then arrest both.

The plan did not go as well as Allan had hoped.

As it turned out, it was a stormy night. Rain was coming down in sheets. Thunder and lightning blanketed the dark sky.

Allan left Terry's when Ben met up with Christine. He had seen this same scenario play out several times before and knew that he had at least an hour before Ben left the bar to go to Shirley's Diner. That was when he decided to leave and go to get a closer look at what was going on behind the restaurant.

Allan decided he wanted a closer look at Kyle, so he pulled into the lot and walked inside, taking a booth near the rear of the building. It was a small diner with six booths and a dozen chairs pulled up to a small counter overlooking the grill.

"What can I get you?" a young server in her late twenties asked. She wore a name tag that read Marsha.

"I'll take a cup of coffee and a cheeseburger with mustard and pickles," he said.

A minute later, the server reappeared with a half-full pot of coffee, and she poured him a cup.

"Nasty night out there, isn't it?" she asked.

"Yes, it is."

"Haven't seen you in here before, what made you decide to stop in?"

"I was visiting a friend and saw your lights on. Guess I was a little hungry, so I decided to stop in. It seems like a nice place."

"It's a hole in the wall, but the food's not bad.

Neither is the coffee," Marsha said with a smile.

There were no other customers at that time. The paint was peeling from the walls, and the entire place looked like it needed a good cleaning. A minute later, the server yelled the order into the cook, and Kyle threw a fresh beef patty down on the grill.

When the burger was done, Marsha brought it over to Allan and sat it down in front of him. The aroma of the patty tickled his nose. Allan took a bite and then a sip of coffee to wash it down. Then he looked at his watch. It was 2:10 am. Allan realized that Ben would be coming in the diner soon. He would certainly recognize Allan. He had to leave quickly before Ben arrived.

It was then that Kyle took a break and went out behind the diner. From what Mason had told him, Allan had a good idea of what was going on.

He finished his burger, threw down a ten dollar bill, and left.

Inside the car, Allan drove a block away, out of sight of the restaurant, and parked his car.

It was then that he came up with a plan to find out what was taking place behind the building. Allan got out of his car, grabbed a tire iron from the trunk, and walked around the back of the diner.

Next to the garbage cans, he saw Kyle and a young man with long hair and dirty clothes. Kyle took money from the stranger and handed him a plastic bag in exchange.

When Kyle went back in the diner, the young man began to leave. That's when Allan approached the young man. Allan showed the tire iron. Hand me the plastic bag," he said. A struggle happened, and Allan grabbed the plastic bag from the man's hands. As he turned to run away, the stranger pulled a knife and stabbed Allan in the back. He realized instantly things had gone terribly wrong.

Allan turned and struck the stranger several times with the tire iron until he dropped the knife. Then he hobbled back to his car and drove away.

Allan, still flush with adrenaline, didn't know how bad the gash was, but he assumed he had been stabbed because he could feel the shooting pain in his back and his shirt sticking to the warm, wet blood.

"Shit," he said out loud as he touched his back with his right hand and pulled it back, exposing a bloody hand.

It was at that very time that Booger and Mason found an unlocked window at Ben's house, opened it, and crawled inside. Their feet were muddy from the rain, and they left footprints inside the house.

The house was completely dark. Mason pulled a flashlight out of his jacket pocket and turned it on. The old wood floor creaked as the two men walked. It was deadly quiet inside except for the sound of rain plummeting against the windows and roof. The two men searched the main floor with no success. Then they went upstairs to the two bedrooms and searched them. Nothing. Finally, they found a locked door on the main floor. Mason used an old credit card to shimmy in the gap and hold back the lock so they could enter. Steep steps led down to a cellar. It was cold and damp. The cellar had brick walls and a dirt floor. There was nothing down there. It was completely empty.

That's when Booger discovered another door, also locked. Mason again used his credit card to open it. Inside was what the two men were hoping to find.

"Shit," Mason said. "It's a meth lab."

In that small 10′x12′ room, the two detectives discovered the source of drugs that Ben and Kyle were peddling. It was a small operation, but it explained the strangers that showed up at Shirley's diner late at night.

At the same time, five miles away, Allan raced to Booger's warehouse and home. Blood was coating the back of his shirt and the seat of his car by the time he arrived.

He got out and walked to the front door, blood dripping on the concrete parking lot as he went. He rang the bell several times before Rose unlocked the front door and let him in.

"Oh, my God," she yelled out when she saw all the blood. "What happened?"

"I guess I was stabbed," Allan replied.

"Let me get you to the bathroom. I've got antibiotics, bandages, and a sewing kit."

Rose had doctored Booger up several times over the years and had become efficient at it.

"It's deep enough that you're going to need stitches," she told Allan.

Booger has some rye whiskey in the man cave. I'll get it. It will help with the pain."

Five large gulps of rye whiskey, and Allan was ready for the stitches. Rose poured a little on the wound before using the stitches.

"Shit," he yelled. "That hurts."

"I'm not a doctor. I won't tell you that you'll experience a little discomfort. You'll be in pain," Rose said. "Take another shot of whiskey if you need it."

"Nah, I'm good."

"How'd you get stabbed?" Rose asked.

"I tried taking drugs away from a dealer."

"That will do it. Lucky, you're still alive. Why don't you leave the dangerous stuff to Booger and Mason?"

"Oh, I thought I could be helpful to them. Mason talked about the plastic bags that were being handed out by Kyle. I figured I could get him one so he could determine what was inside."

After cleaning the wound and stitching it, Rose bandaged it and gave Allan two amoxicillin. Then she helped him to bed.

The whiskey had done the trick. Allan said he hardly felt a thing once she got going. Fifteen minutes after he was bandaged up, Allan was sound asleep.

That's when Rose called Booger. "Sweetie, you need to come home. Allan was stabbed outside Shirley's Diner."

"What? How?"

"He was playing detective. He evidently crossed paths with a drug dealer in an attempt to get a plastic bag of drugs that Kyle had given to the guy."

"Oh, shit. Why would he do that?"

"I think he wanted to impress you and Mason."

"Did he get the drugs?"

"Yes, he handed them to me before he went to bed."

"So, he's okay?"

"Yeah, I bandaged him up. He'll be a little sore in the morning but he's just fine. You might want to pick up some more rye whiskey, though. He nearly polished off a full quart. I think you're about out."

"Umm, yeah," Booger said, thinking of the three pints he had hidden in his office. "I wouldn't want to run out."

CHAPTER 14
THE MOUSE BECOMES THE CAT

A dealer-plated blue Chevrolet pulled into the lot at Booger's warehouse three minutes after Allan arrived. It parked near the lot entrance and watched as Rose opened the door for Allan and let him in.

Ben had spotted Allan as he left the diner. He followed him to Booger's. "Bam! I knew it. I knew I'd seen her at the dealership with those detectives. What are they doing? What do they think they know? And now she's with Allan?"

His questions about them would only increase when he got to Shirley's Diner.

"We've been robbed," Kyle said.

"What are you talking about?"

"An old man came in the diner tonight. When he left, he went around back. He must have spotted me with one of my dealers. He must have seen the drugs changing hands. When I went back inside, he jumped my associate and took the drugs."

"Shit, I think I know who it was."

"Who?"

"My father-in-law. Well, ex-father-in-law. I saw him leave here, and I followed him. He drove to a warehouse on the north side. I watched as he got out of the car and went to the front door. He was bleeding. I think your guy must have stabbed him."

"Yeah, he said there was blood on his knife. Do you think he's hurt bad?"

"I don't think so. He seemed to be walking okay. Anyway, I recognized the lady who came to the front door. She has been in Terry's Tavern several times. She sat at the bar next to me. We talked and flirted, but I couldn't get her to come home with me. I know she's working with a couple of detectives. Well, and my father-in-law, too, apparently."

"Well, they were after drugs last night. At least your father-in-law was. Does he know you have a twin?"

"He might now."

"Well, we need to take care of them before they do us any more harm."

"No, it's my problem," Ben said. "I'll take care of them."

"How's your guy?"

"He's fine. We lost an eight ball. It's no big deal. Just annoying."

"Damn. It's okay. I'll get it back."

When he arrived home that morning, he saw the muddy footprints in his house. The rain from the night before had caused Booger and Mason's shoes to get muddy, so when they crawled through the window and onto the floor, they left muddy prints.

Based on the different sizes of prints, Ben knew there were two different people in his house. Nothing appeared to be stolen, and the meth lab was undisturbed, but footprints were inside.

"Damn, they know where my lab is."

"Kyle, they've been in my house, two of them," he said on the cellphone. "We need to meet."

"In the apartment?"

"No, let's meet in the park down from your apartment in case someone is listening in. I'll be there in fifteen minutes."

The two brothers met on a bench at Phelps Grove Park in the park twenty minutes later.

"Do you think it was the woman and old man who broke into your house?"

"No, I don't think so. The footprints are too large for a woman. I think it was two men."

"Did they take anything?"

"No. I think it was a hunting expedition," Ben said. "I don't like it. They know too much."

"So, one member of the gang takes drugs from my guy, and two others get into your lab and don't take anything?"

"Right."

"You sure nothing was missing?"

"I'm sure."

"Do you think they bugged the place?"

"I don't know. It's possible. I looked around but didn't see anything."

"The weird thing is that they had to know that they left footprints and that I would know they had been in the house."

"Yeah, what do you make of that?"

"I think they wanted me to know they were there."

"Why?"

"Maybe they're trying to scare me."

"Well, regardless, they know where your lab is now. You have to move it."

"Yes, I know."

"Jarvis should be able to help."

"Jarvis?"

"My guy, you know? Umm, we visited you in Wichita. Ring any bells?"

"Oh, right. I'm not thinking clearly. Jesus, how long have you known him?"

"Forever. He and I used to run around together when I lived with Grandma. He was the adopted son of her neighbor. After Grandma died, he and I lived together for a few months. He's got a place on the northwest side. It's not much, but he cooks downstairs and has a pretty decent network of runners. His operation is about ten times the size of ours. He can give us a place to cook and offer us some protection."

"Yeah, but what would he want in return?"

"Probably do it for a cut of the action. Maybe he'll want us to go under his umbrella. It doesn't matter. We're like family. He'll take care of us."

"Is it safe?"

"I'm pretty sure he has a police connection that helps keep him off the DEA's radar. They don't bother him, and he's got muscle, so if anyone tried to interfere with his operation."

"I don't know, Kyle. You know that I never have

been into drugs. It's not my thing. I'm only involved in it because I owe you, you know?"

"What? For getting you outta Wichita? For pulling you out of that lake. You paid me back long ago, bro."

"Yeah, I suppose."

"I figured by now you were in it for the income. You make a hell of a lot more selling drugs than you do selling cars. You're not much of a salesman."

"Yeah, but it's never been my intention to do it for this long. This is your thing. Not mine."

"And you can walk away from it whenever you want."

"Yes. I just might once you're set up with Jarvis."

"What about your girlfriend, Christine? Anything going to happen there?"

"I don't know. I think the only reason she cares about me is the meth I give her. She's wealthy, you know. Not sure she'd want to go dumpster diving with someone like me. The sex is great, though."

"Why don't you cut her off? Maybe then you'll find out if she really cares about you or the drugs."

"I can't do that. She's hooked on it now."

"Yeah, you wouldn't want to do anything immoral?" Kyle said with a laugh. Before Ben could respond, Kyle asked, "What are you going to do if you get out of the meth business? I'm sure as hell not going to supply you with free shit for you to give to your girlfriend."

"I know. Maybe it's time to get out, though. We've got detectives following us. That's what we should be focused on."

There was a moment of silence where both brothers were lost in thought. "Are you sure that you don't want my help taking care of the people that broke into your house?" Kyle asked.

"I'm sure. It's my problem. But, if the problem is more than I can handle, I'll let you know."

"Thanks."

———

In the days that followed, Ben started being more cautious. He never saw Booger's car, but he suspected someone was watching. As a precaution, whenever he needed to leave his house, he slipped out the back and jogged, always being careful to stay away from the street out front of the household. Mostly, where he jogged to was Booger's warehouse, where he would find a place in the woods out behind to keep an eye on the building.

It didn't take him long to notice that Rose was the only one in the warehouse late in the afternoon and early evening. During the mornings, three men were there, but by 4 pm, they were gone, and Rose was alone.

He didn't know it, but Booger and Mason were watching his house late in the afternoon and evening, and Allan was watching Kyle's apartment. He had parked his car in his driveway and turned on the lights in the house, which gave the appearance that he was home. By 9 pm, he jogged back home and by 10 pm, he followed his normal routine and left in his car for Terry's Tavern.

In Booger's mind, Ben was following the same routine as before. Rose was unaware that she was being watched.

"You thought you could hunt the hunter?" Ben said to himself from the wooded shadows near Booger's office. "Big mistake."

CHAPTER 15
KYLE'S STORY

Ben and Kyle Squires were born in Farmington, Missouri, in 1975. It was a difficult birth for Janie Collins, one that left her unable to carry more children. Kyle was born first, followed by Ben two minutes later.

From birth, they were inseparable, doing everything together. In school, they sat next to each other. At recess, they played together. They were each other's best friends.

As they reached their teenage years, it seemed obvious that although they were twins, they were very different. Kyle was constantly getting into trouble. Ben was the good child, and the parents awarded each accordingly. Kids at school called Kyle the "bad twin." Ben was the good one. His parents showed an unconscious favoritism toward Ben. With time, Kyle got blamed for more than he should have, and he acted out more, accordingly. Ben fed off the attention he got – especially from his mother, as his dad was often drunk at home.

At the age of thirteen, Kyle began breaking into homes, stealing, and drinking. Still, Ben looked up to his "older" brother. In his mind, Kyle could do nothing wrong. There were plenty of times when Kyle tried to involve Ben in some of his criminal activities, but he always resisted. Though they were treated differently, they remained close. They held between them a secret: Ben wasn't as good as everyone thought, and Kyle wasn't as bad. They each, for reasons they'd never fully understand, enjoyed people's misperceptions about them. They could play their roles and protect their true identities.

That was until the day Tina Mae Cooks disappeared. Nathan Williamson, seventeen, came to town from Sikeston to visit his friend, Kyle. They had been roommates at the Southern Missouri Juvenile Detention Center, a place Kyle was sent after being caught breaking into a neighbor's house.

Nathan brought beer and persuaded Kyle to go out cruising with him and a friend he brought with him named Tim. Kyle asked his brother to come along against his mother's wishes.

"We're just going to cruise around," Kyle said. "Come with us."

Ben didn't hesitate. He told his mother that everything would be fine. He welcomed an opportunity to spend time with his brother and friends.

What Ben didn't know was that his brother's friend, Nathan, was a sexual deviant who had more in mind than just cruising around drinking beer. He, flanked by his buddy Tim, were hunting for an attractive young girl. The more the group drank, the more they became willing to play along with whatever Nathan wanted.

As fate would have it, Kyle wouldn't be in the car

that evening when they spotted Tina on her bicycle. Just fifteen minutes earlier, the boys cruised by the home of Cindy Freatis, Kyle's girlfriend.

"Let me out," he said. "I want to talk to Cindy."

Tim, who was driving the car, stopped and let Kyle out. "I'll see you back at the house in thirty minutes," he said to his brother, saying in an unspoken way that he wanted time alone with Cindy. "Tim, can you drop Ben off at the house before 11 pm? That's his curfew."

"Sure," Tim said.

But Nathan had other plans.

Whether he wanted to be involved or not, after Nathan asked Tim to pull over in front of Tina's bicycle, once Nathan grabbed her from the streets, Ben's life changed forever.

Tina Mae Cooks was raped and murdered and left in the woods north of Fredericktown, near an abandoned quarry. All three boys had a hand in what happened; Nathan made sure of that. Ben hadn't wanted her to die, and as he'd told his brother a dozen times – he shouldn't have been in that car. But he was, and she had.

When Ben arrived home at nearly 2 am, his shirt covered in blood, his mother was furious. He would confess everything to her. His mother cried and was completely distraught. In the days that followed, both parents would blame Kyle for what happened. After all, Ben was the good son. If not for Kyle, Ben would never have been in Nathan's station wagon.

The parents protected Ben. They told him what to say if the police ever questioned him. As luck would have, it wouldn't matter. Sherriff Parras was convinced that teenagers from St. Louis came down to attack Tina.

Still, Janie believed investigators would figure out what happened eventually, so she insisted the family move. That was when they made the decision to send Kyle away to his paternal grandmother's house in Springfield. He would live with her and be out of sight, out of mind. Janie felt they couldn't save Kyle, but at least they could protect Ben. Then, they'd never speak of what happened again. It was how they dealt with it. That's when the Squires family moved to Wichita and became the Collins family.

But they underestimated how close the two brothers were and how determined they were to communicate with each other. They called each other when no one else was around. Later, they'd email. When they got older, Ben would visit his grandmother in Springfield when he could, and Kyle traveled to Wichita to see his brother, too.

Kyle's grandmother wasn't much of a guardian. She let Kyle come and go as he pleased. He dropped out of school and got heavily involved in drugs. His friends were drug addicts. His drug of choice was meth. He learned how to make it from his neighbor friend, Jarvis Duechene, who had almost no adult supervision. Together, for a time, they produced the dangerous drug in the basement of an abandoned house on the northwest side of town.

It was a small operation, but what meth they didn't use themselves, they sold on the streets and to other drug addicts. It provided Kyle with plenty of spending money to buy a car and make his periodic trips to Wichita to visit his brother.

Kyle's dark side was drugs. He would do anything to get them. There was a time when he was in his early twenties when a drug addict customer of his stole a stash of meth from Kyle. He tracked the culprit down and cut off his right hand with a machete. No one messed with Kyle's drugs after that.

Ben became obsessed with protecting his identity as a good person. He felt he couldn't afford for anyone to see his dark side. He was also alone in trying to process what had happened in Park Hills. Ben had been a virgin before he participated in the rape of Gina. He had tried to fight it, but Nathan held a gun to his head that night. "We're in this together, you idiot. You're going to fuck her, too. And then you're going to help kill her. You're not the good one anymore," Nathan said, laughing.

After Ben moved to Wichita, he relished his new identity as Wade Collins. It was a chance to start over. But he could never escape his past. His dreams were tortured. And as a byproduct of his past, he considered his own sexual desires evil. They were a thing to be hidden. Violence and sex were twisted vines entangled and set in his puberty.

If Kyle's Achilles' heel was drugs, Ben's was sex.

While his mother was still alive, Ben managed to keep his dark side at bay. That was until his father was killed. That's when he couldn't hide his evil desires anymore. That's when things started falling apart. He started seeing his good and bad sides as wholly separate. When he found his mother's diary, he found targets for his evil impulses. His mother, he thought, had been corrupted by his bad father. Because his father wasn't there, she had become sexually active. She gave into her dark side.

That's why Ben was fixated on red dresses. His mother wore them.

After his mother's death, Ben would often go into bars looking for women wearing a red dress or married men hitting on women. Several became his victims. Over time, Ben, giving into his dark side, sought the women in red dresses for himself.

Kyle learned of his brother's demons one time when he came to Wichita. They had gotten drunk at a bar, and Ben told his twin everything. Between the two, there was no judgment. Kyle was addicted to the speed he pushed, and though he initially tried to encourage his brother to get counseling, it was no use. Ben, once or twice, had told his brother he needed rehab. His heart wasn't in it, though. The truth was complicated. They both were broken by the weight of the shame they carried. They both had gone off the right path and just kept going. The only thing they knew was how to hide the truth. Not even his wife of ten years knew about Kyle. Ben had gone to great links to keep their occasional meetings a secret. It was part of a life he never wanted her to know.

For these brothers, the only thing that really mattered in the whole world was each other. When Ben needed someone to help him finish burying his wife because he wasn't fully recovered from his car accident, Kyle was there. When Kyle needed a place for his lab, Ben didn't hesitate to help. They were everything to each other. And no, Nathan would never get between them again.

CHAPTER 16

JARVIS DUNCAN

Jarvis Duechene looked like a junkie – bone thin, dark eyes, rotten teeth. He had lived a difficult life. He never knew his father. His mother was a junkie who often slept around with strange men. He largely raised himself, though the older neighbor lady – Kyle's grandma – often looked out for him and would feed him if he started looking too thin.

Three years older than Kyle, Jarvis was a mentor, so to speak. He had shown Kyle the ropes in the speed game. They were close in the way of thieves. There was an unspoken bond between them. They had shared the same addiction, the same struggles, and the same deep feeling that life had handed them bad cards.

Jarvis grew up on the wrong side of town. His mother was rarely around and died three days before he turned twenty-one. By then, he'd been addicted to meth and gone to jail twice for drug possession. As he got older, he'd learn how to avoid jail.

He began cooking before his 20th birthday. What he didn't use himself or share with friends like Kyle, he sold on the streets. In his early thirties, he was making about $10,000 a month working out of a rundown house on the northwest side of town.

"The key to not getting caught is to have other people sell for you," Jarvis told Kyle once. "It's also important to be ready at any given time for your house to be raided. It doesn't matter if the cops know you're selling. It matters if they can prove it. Luckily, I know a guy on the inside."

Kyle bought meth from Jarvis for a time when they were young, but Jarvis had taught Kyle how to make it himself. This way, Kyle could be independent. It wasn't something Jarvis did with just anyone because then no one would buy from him. Still, it wasn't alien to the culture, either. It is a sign of deep respect to teach someone how to make on their own. To teach someone means they are like family. It is like sharing a dark secret no one can know.

"Someone has stolen from us and has broken into our meth lab. I don't know what to do," Kyle told his old friend after the incident at his brother's home.

"I can help," Jarvis said, without hesitation.

Jarvis was glad to assist, but it meant his friend would need to come under his umbrella, for a time at least. He'd open up the lab for Kyle to cook, but they would turn all sales over to Jarvis, and he would pay a percentage back to Kyle. It was a small price to pay, Kyle thought.

After all, by this point in his life, Jarvis had a fairly large organization that included dozens of runners and three enforcers. He could provide Kyle the protection he needed.

Kyle signed on with his friend, and the small meth

lab in Ben's house was shut down. Ben wasn't interested in that arrangement. He didn't trust Jarvis. Truth be told, he was happy to get out of the drug business. His only concern was Christine. They had been lovers for a couple of years now. She was hooked by this point and needed her nightly fix.

When he met with her and told her that he would no longer be supplying her, she was visibly upset.

"You son of a bitch!" she shouted. "You can't just cut me off."

The sex stopped immediately. She had no interest in feeding Ben's needs if he wasn't feeding hers. Christine was wealthy. She could afford to pay for her drugs and could find somewhere else to get them. The sex was good, but he never expected his secret rendezvous with her to go anyplace, and the small hope he had that she actually cared about him was dashed when she walked away that night. Because he had dealt to her and had been seen with her public on multiple occasions, she would never be introduced to his shadow self. Truth be told, it was the simplest, most honest, and fulfilling relationship Ben had ever been in.

That said, this turn of events allowed Ben to focus his attention on something he felt he had neglected for too long: the problem of his father-in-law. He knew Allan suspected him of killing his daughter and wife. Ben was all but certain Allan was the one who had interfered with his drug lab – and thereby cost him his most cherished lover. Plus, he posed a threat legally. Ben couldn't have Allan figuring out how to prove the truth of what happened to his wife and daughter. Ben's path was clear: he needed to kill Allan.

More than that, he needed to kill these people who were helping Allan: the three detectives who'd visited him at the car lot. He couldn't afford to have any loose ends out there, to have anything come back on Kyle or his meth-dealing friend, so he continued to watch the group and to plan an attack. He knew it would be difficult to take all four at one time, so he decided he needed to focus on one first.

That was Rose. She was alone in that house in the late afternoon and evening. He would attack her when the men were away. That would be fun, he thought. Then, when the others came for him, he could pick them off one at a time. So, Ben's plan began to take shape.

"Are you sure you don't want help, little brother?" Kyle said.

"No, I can handle it myself," Ben said. "Look, if anything goes wrong – and I don't expect it to – you've got to look out for yourself. You've got to finish it, right?"

"Right."

Truthfully, Ben was looking forward to this. He was excited, in fact. It seemed murder was an acquired taste, and he had acquired it by now.

"Well, there is one thing, Kyle. I need you to continue the same routine every night, knowing that they will be watching you and me. I don't want them to think anything is different."

"Sure. No problem."

So, Kyle and his girlfriend went to work at

Shirley's Diner every night like they used to. Everything appeared to return to normal. Ben left for Terry's Tavern every night at about the same time. He took a seat at the bar and flirted with women, even taking some out to his car for a quickie once in a while. It was enough to keep Booger at the bar, watching him.

The rouse worked as planned.

Ben knew Booger was tracking him late in the afternoons and early evenings. Once he started looking for someone watching his house and monitoring Ben at the dealership, it wasn't difficult to spot Booger's red Corvette down the street in nearly the same spot every day.

Kyle worked noon to 8 pm four days a week. Knowing exactly where Booger's car was made it easy for Ben to slip away from work in a new demo car. With Booger still staking out the car dealership, Ben drove to Booger's warehouse. It was around 5 pm when Ben parked in a vacant lot across from the warehouse. From there he walked to the back of the building to the sliding glass door of the house where Rose and Booger lived. A thin metal tool was used to break the lock and get inside. Ben searched every part of the house. Rose wasn't there, so he went into the warehouse and headed up the stairs to the offices.

On the third floor in Booger's office, he saw Rose sitting at her desk, reading a magazine. Suddenly, the phone rang.

It was Booger on the other line.

"Something's wrong," he said. "It's Tuesday. Ben

is usually at his desk from 7 until 8. It's 7:30 now, and I haven't seen him in over a half hour. Is everything okay there?"

"Yes, I'm fine. You don't think he's coming here, do you?"

"No, I don't, but just in case, keep the gun close by and keep an eye on the video monitors."

"Oh, okay. I've just been here reading."

"Yeah, I'm probably just being paranoid."

It was then that the glass on the office door shattered, and Rose saw Ben sticking his hand through the opening to unlock the door.

She screamed into the phone, "He's here!"

Booger panicked and yelled back, "Get the gun! I'm on my way."

Booger sped away from the car dealership and raced toward home, ignoring stop signs and lights.

Rose opened her desk drawer and pulled out her 44-revolver. She lifted it as the intruder raced toward her.

"I've got a gun. I'll shoot you if I have to," she yelled.

Ben did a quick calculation before he ignored her and continued forward. He reasoned that the gun would be unloaded. Most people don't keep a loaded gun in their desk. Secondly, he was the attacker. She was the one who was scared and nervous. If he stopped, he'd be relinquishing control of the situation. She was feet away. He thought, *I need to get that gun.*

She pulled the safety and fired one, two, three shots. Not more than five feet from her, Ben fell to the ground.

The last thing he saw was the flash of the gun. The last thing he felt was the violent heat of the bullet before everything went black.

It took Booger eight minutes to get home. He raced inside and up the stairs. When he got to the office, he found Rose, hysterical, shaking.

"Are you alright, sweetie?"

"No," she said with her voice shaking. "I think I killed him."

When the police came, Booger did his best to explain that they believed Ben was the local killer they'd been looking for. Mason came back to the office to add credibility to his story.

"We've been tracking this guy and his brother for weeks," Booger said.

"I've been on this psycho's trail for years. I took a leave so I could come here and see if he was still killing. It's the same guy from Wichita. This is a true serial killer," Mason told the detective. "He's got a twin too. The guy's name is Kyle. He's dealing meth out of the back of Shirley's. We've been monitoring both of them for a couple of weeks."

Booger's system had recorded Ben's entry and the shooting in the office. Booger turned over the tapes to the police. Detective Derek Johnson told the trio he'd be in touch.

"Looks like a clear case of self-defense here. As for the recent murders, we will keep things in-house for now," Johnson said, meaning there'd be no immediate announcement to the media. "We need to run fingerprints and see if we can truly connect this guy to the murders. You understand."

"Of course," Booger and Mason said, simultaneously.

Rose was shaken up by everything. She didn't sleep that night and was barely able to get out of bed the next day.

The office would need a thorough cleaning. There was shattered glass and blood stains on the floor. She kept playing the shooting over and over in her mind.

"Let's take a few days off, sweetie," Booger said. "Until the cleaning crew replaces the carpet and glass door, we can't work out of the office, anyway."

Booger paid for hotel rooms at University Plaza for him and his wife, Mason, and Allan. Three days after the shooting, he called a meeting with the four of them at George's Steakhouse. Booger insisted Rose come along so that she wasn't left out.

"I talked with Johnson again. The police are assuming the killer was Wade Collins – well, you know, Ben Sawyers – and are closing the case. The detective in charge is satisfied that Rose killed their guy," Mason said.

"Damn right I did," she said.

"They said they'll make an announcement soon but plan to keep Rose's identity anonymous," Mason added. "According to the chief, 'we can't have anyone else burning down your house.'"

"That would be nice," she said, looking at her husband.

"I have to admit, that's funny," Booger said with a grin. "Any news on Kyle?"

"You know how it goes. He's been arrested before for meth, and they've suspected he's a dealer for a while. They're gonna put surveillance on him, but who knows. The murders were the priority and that parts over. He asked if I believed Kyle was involved, and I said, 'no.' He nodded, and so I'm sure that means they're not really worried about him. He told me to keep him posted if we learned anything new."

"I guess this pretty much wraps it up for both of you," Booger said to Mason and Allan. "Ben is dead. I don't imagine you will want to hang around much longer."

Allan nodded in agreement. "Yeah, the son of bitch is dead. That's all I ever wanted," he said with a bit of a snort to hold back any potential tears. "I've had my fun being a detective, but I'm done. I need to get back to the farm where I belong."

"Yeah, it's almost time for me to get back. I've stayed longer than I planned to, but if you don't mind, I'd like to stay another couple of days," Mason said. "Given everything, my boss has extended my vacation, and I wouldn't mind keeping an eye on Kyle with you guys. I wanna know what he does now with his brother gone."

"Of course!" Rose said before Booger could answer, giving Mason a big hug. She then turned to Allan and gave him one as well.

"Thanks," Allan said, smiling. He then shook hands with Mason and Booger. "Good luck to all y'all.

I really mean it. And anytime you want, you all are welcome out to the farm."

They all thanked him and wished him goodbye. After Allan's final wave, Mason, Booger, and Rose sat back down to finish their coffee. Mason looked like he had something on his mind, and so Rose asked him, "What's going on? Are you okay?"

"Yeah, I'm fine. You know, I guess there's always been one thing that bothers me about Wade."

"What's that?" Booger asked.

"The cigarettes."

"What?"

"In Wichita, after I chased him down and thought I'd killed him, someone left a calling card for me in the woods by a tree within eyesight of my cabin. I found fresh cigarette butts. I thought Wade was a chain smoker but that just didn't add up. He was a bit of a health nut that jogged every day. He didn't smoke. His brother Kyle smoked. He is the chain smoker."

"The two were twins. They looked alike and had many of the same mannerisms. Is it possible we mistook one brother for the other?" Booger asked.

"No, I don't think so," Mason said. "It's best we not to overthink things. We followed them from their homes to work. Someone would have noticed if they switched places."

"Maybe, maybe not. Remember how every night Wade drove his brother and girlfriend home? He was in that apartment for a long time, then drove home. Maybe they switched places. No one would have noticed,"

Booger said.

"Yeah, but it's one thing for them to switch places at the diner late at night. It's something else to switch places in front of people who know you, like the employees at the car dealership where Wade worked. And what about his lover Christine and Kyle's girlfriend? Are you saying they couldn't tell which brother was which? I just don't believe it's possible for identical twins to switch places in front of people who are very familiar with you and get away with it."

"Let's just suppose for a minute that Kyle was the evil brother and that Wade was the good brother?" Booger speculated. "They switched places in Wichita after Wade's mother died. Parents would have been able to tell one twin from the other when most people could not. Wade would have gone back to Springfield and stayed with the grandmother. Kyle would have begun the killing spree in Wichita.

"Well, it's possible," Mason said. "It doesn't seem likely to me, but it would explain the cigarettes."

"Then which brother is laying in the city morgue right now? Is it Wade or Kyle?" Rose asked

"I don't know," Booger said.

"You mean the person who killed over a dozen people could still be alive?"

"Yes."

By the time the three were paying their tab at George's, Allan was adjusting his rear-view mirror as he headed north out of Springfield on Highway 13. The car behind him was driving aggressively and had its brights on.

"What are you doing, jerk?" Allan murmured to himself. Then, just north of the landfill, the beat-up Chevy pickup truck swerved into the passing lane. The driver coasted parallel to Allan for a moment before the face of his son-in-law waved at him. It would be the last thing Allan ever saw.

The next morning, Missouri Highway Patrol would find the farmer in a ravine off the side of Hwy. 13 in the mangled wreck of his vehicle.

CHAPTER 17
THE CABIN

The phone rang. The call was for Booger. Few words were said. The conversation was short and to the point. When Booger got off the phone, he lit a stogie, poured a glass of rye whiskey, and leaned back in his chair to contemplate the call he just received.

"What's wrong?" Rose asked. Pouring a glass of whiskey at nine in the morning was out of character for Booger as was him being silent.

"Call Mason in here, please, Rose."

"Okay."

When Mason arrived both Rose and Mason took a seat in Booger's office.

Booger poured another glass of whiskey for Mason.

"No thanks, buddy. It's a little early in the day for me."

"Drink it," Booger said. "You're going to need it with the news I have to tell you."

Mason took a sip. "What is it, Booger?"

"Allan's dead."

Rose let out a gasp.

"No, it can't be," Mason said.

"Drove off the side of the hill past the landfill on 13. Police don't suspect foul play, but I sure as hell do,"

Booger said, followed by another shot of whiskey. "And that's not all."

"What do you mean?" Mason asked, almost yelling.

"I got an email from the detective who's been working with the FBI. It appears the fingerprints in the Wichita killings don't exactly match Wade or Kyle.

"What?" Rose said even louder than Mason.

"What does that mean?" Booger asked. "Neither brother committed the crimes?"

"No, it means the fingerprints we lifted off of the mother's diary in Wichita, as well as the cigarettes near the lake – which were an exact match – didn't belong to the twins," Mason said. "But they did belong to a close relative."

"What?!" Rose yelled.

"How could that be?" Booger asked

"I don't know. The DNA was very close to a match. So close that the FBI believes the killer was a close relative to Kyle and Wade. Possibly a half-brother."

"Shit. You have to be kidding me," Booger said.

Mason took another drag from his cigar and finished off the tall glass of whiskey. "Unbelievable. I think we need to keep a close eye on Kyle. Maybe he'll lead us to the relative."

"There is another problem, too," Booger said. "It's very possible that whoever killed Allan will also be coming for us. If the motive was revenge for the death of Ben, I doubt they'd stop with Allan. All three of us could be targets."

Rose sat back in her chair. "It's 5 pm somewhere. Better give me a glass of that whiskey, too."

"Rose, sweetie, I want you to stay put here. Keep a close eye on the video monitors in the parking lot and surrounding areas. If you see anything suspicious, call me immediately. Mason, one of us will be here with Rose at all times. We'll rotate 12-hour shifts watching Kyle. Whoever is not watching Kyle will stay with Rose. Is that clear?"

"Yes, that makes sense."

"The office is like a fortress. Surveillance cameras are positioned toward every corner of the area outside the building. If anyone approaches, they will be on camera. Likewise, there are video cameras covering most of the inside of the building. Someone needs to be watching those cameras at all times. We'll sleep in shifts, so someone is always awake to watch."

"If someone does get inside, we have a safe room on the second floor. Get to that room and stay there. Inside is a direct line to the police. Call them and wait for help."

"Sounds like a plan," Mason said.

That evening, they began their shifts. Booger took the first shift watching Kyle. He drove to Kyle's apartment and watched. Nothing happened until after 9 pm. That's when Kyle and his girlfriend left the apartment and went to Shirley's Diner. Booger followed them to work. He watched through binoculars as the two worked.

"Anything happen?" Mason asked at the change of shifts.

"No. In fact, Kyle didn't meet up with anyone. He took several smoking breaks out back of the diner, but he met with no one. There were no exchanges of drugs."

Mason took the day shift watching Kyle's apartment. There was nothing for Mason to report that first day, or the second day, or the third day. Same for Booger on the night shift. Kyle simply worked his shift, went back to the apartment, and stayed there. If an errand needed to be run, the girlfriend did it. It was as if Kyle knew he was being watched. And it didn't look like he was dealing drugs at all anymore.

It was on the fourth day of their surveillance that things changed.

Mason was watching the apartment that day and saw nothing unusual. Booger took over the shift at 8 pm. At approximately 9:30 pm, the girlfriend left the apartment, got in the car, and left. This was their usual time for going to work. But there was no sign of Kyle. The girlfriend was alone. The lights went off in the apartment when she left, and there was no sign of Kyle. He simply disappeared.

Booger stayed outside the apartment for two hours, waiting to see if there was any movement inside. There wasn't. At nearly midnight, he drove to Shirley's Diner. Inside, he saw the girlfriend, but the cook that was behind the counter wasn't Kyle. It was someone else.

Kyle was nowhere to be found.

"He simply disappeared," Booger said. "Did you see anything out of the ordinary?"

"No. He never left the apartment at least he didn't

through the front entrance."

"Then he is either still inside the apartment, or he left through the back and didn't take the car."

"We need to check the apartment tonight after the girlfriend leaves for work," Booger added.

"Let me go, too, Booger," Rose said. "You can search a lot faster with all three of us. Besides, I don't want to be left all alone."

"I didn't plan on leaving you, Rose. But I don't want you searching the apartment either. You can come, but I need you to wait in the car and watch. If anyone approaches the apartment, text me."

"Okay," Rose said.

That night, Mason watched as the girlfriend left for work and turned out the lights of the apartment. When she was gone, Mason called Booger to let him know. Fifteen minutes later, Booger and Rose pulled up in the red Corvette.

"Let's wait an hour until nearly everyone is asleep, and then we'll break in," Booger said as the three huddled just outside Booger's car.

"What are you boys looking for?" Rose asked.

"Any sign of Kyle or a clue to where he might be."

"How are you going to get in?" Rose asked.

"With this handy tool," Booger said, pulling a thin, flat metal tool out of his jacket pocket.

An hour later, Booger and Mason left the car to walk to the apartment.

"Rose, look out for anyone walking toward the apartment or anything out of the ordinary. If you see something, text me."

"Yes, dear," Rose said with a sarcastic tone.

The lock on the apartment door was a simple one, easy for Booger to penetrate with his metal tool. Once inside, the two detectives pulled out flashlights and began looking through each room of the apartment. Mason was the first to spot the note written on a piece of paper on the nightstand. It contained a phone number.

That was the only clue the duo found in the apartment. A man's clothes were left hanging in the closet, as was a razor, cologne, and other male necessities in the bathroom. There were signs that Kyle had been there recently but no sign he had been there in the last few days.

With only the phone number as a clue, they left the apartment and headed home.

"What did you find?" Rose asked.

"Just a phone number, not even sure who it goes to."

"Are you going to call it?"

"Not yet. First, I want to cross-reference it with addresses and see who the phone number belongs to."

The phone number belonged to a cabin at the lake just outside of Springfield. The phone number was registered to Ben Sawyers. A check of property records indicated the cabin was owned by Ben also.

That was when the trio planned a trip to the cabin the next evening. They needed to know if Kyle was staying there.

That night was a rainy, stormy evening. Fog

limited visibility to just a few feet. The trio took Booger's car and drove the twelve miles north of town to the cabin on the lake. Booger parked a hundred yards away down a dirt road.

"Stay in the car, Rose. Text me if you see anyone."

Booger and Kyle walked through the mud, rain, and fog to a tree line about thirty feet from the cabin. From there, they had good visibility of the cabin. A single light was on inside, and the shades were open. They watched for nearly an hour for any sign of movement. There was nothing.

Suddenly, a light emerged from the back of the cabin. It wasn't a normal light, though. It flickered and got brighter with a little time.

"Shit, it's a fire," Booger yelled.

Booger and Mason ran toward the cabin door. The door was unlocked. They hurried inside. That's when they saw the body on the cabin floor.

"Shit, it's Kyle," Mason yelled.

Just as he started to approach the body, flames swirled near it. That was when Booger saw the propane tanks, four of them lined up at the wall of fire.

He grabbed Mason's arm, preventing him from going any closer. "We've got to get out of here now," he said.

The two detectives ran for the front door. Mason got out first, followed by Booger. They had just reached the porch when the explosion took place. Both men were hurled through the area and landed on the ground twenty feet away from the burning cabin.

Miraculously, both Booger and Mason were all right.

"We've got to get back to the car," Booger said, concerned that his wife would fear the worst after seeing the fire and hearing the explosion.

Booger's ankle was twisted in the fall, so Mason helped him to his feet and walked him to the car.

"Rose, we're all right," Mason said a few feet from the car.

There was no answer.

"Rose," Booger hollered louder now.

There was no response.

When they reached the car and opened the door, Rose was not there.

She had vanished.

CHAPTER 18
THE HOUSE ON MONROE STREET

The phone rang at 8 pm the next evening.

"We have your wife. Come only with Mason tonight at midnight. 412 E. Monroe. Come unarmed." Then, the caller hung up.

"Did you recognize the voice?" Mason asked.

"No."

"What's the plan."

"No plan. You and I are going there to get Rose."

"But it's obviously a trap."

"Yeah, I know, but we've got to go alone and unarmed if we're going to get Rose. You don't have to come if you don't want to. I'll understand, Mason."

"No, nothing's going to keep me from going with you. We need to find out who killed Kyle."

"Well, I've got a bit of a plan, but we need to talk it through."

It was a stormy, rainy night with a hanging fog that worked in the favor of the two detectives. Despite warnings to come unarmed, both Booger and Mason carried firearms. Booger had his strapped to his back so he could reach behind and grab it if needed but otherwise looked unarmed facing front. Mason had his holster just inside his jacket, but if things went the way they hoped, no one would be the wiser until it was too late.

Booger drove his car and parked several blocks away. The two detectives walked the remainder of the way. The house was a small ranch house with a carport. It had a basement.

"We should work our way to the side of the house where there aren't any windows," Booger said.

They moved with the thunder and fell to the ground with the lightning so as not to be seen. There were three windows leading to the basement. At one window, Mason used a glass cutting tool to cut a circular hole at the base of the window. Then he reached in and unlocked it. With the window fully opened, Booger and he climbed inside the completely dark basement. They felt their way around the four walls until they found an opening in one of the walls. The opening was a tunnel cut into the earth. Booger climbed in while Mason kept the lookout. The tunnel went down into the earth at about a 45-degree angle. Fifteen yards into it, he felt a wire cage in front of him. It was too dark to see if anyone or anything was inside the cage. The door was securely locked and impossible to open without the key or bolt cutters, neither of which Booger had.

Rain was coming in from the ground above, and with his fingers extended through the wire cage, he could feel about two inches of water that had accumulated at the base of the cage, making the dirt floor a muddy mess.

"Rose, are you in there?" he whispered.

There was no response.

"Rose, are you in there?" He said in a louder voice.

"Mmmph," was the only response.

"Are you okay?"

"Mm-hmm."

Booger guessed his wife's mouth was taped. "I'll be back to get you soon, sweetie. Hang in there."

Then Booger backed up through the tunnel to the basement.

"She's in there," Booger whispered to Mason "but the lock is too strong to open it without the key or bolt cutters."

"What are we going to do?" Mason asked.

"We're going to get the key," Booger replied.

"Do you have that gadget you use to open locked doors? Booger asked.

"Yes, I have it."

"Good."

"Wait exactly five minutes and then use it to unlock the basement door. That is if it's locked, which I figure it is. But don't go in the house until you hear gunfire. Then take out as many of them as you can while I distract them from the front of the house."

With the rain pouring down, Booger climbed outside the window and moved toward the front of the house using the tree line to stay hidden from view. About fifty feet from the front of the house, Booger began moving toward it. As he got closer, he could see the eyes looking toward him through openings in the drapes covering the three windows at the front of the house.

He slowly moved closer and closer to the house, the lightening illuminating every movement. As he got to the porch, the door suddenly opened, and Jarvis stood there pointing a 45-revolver at him.

Booger held his hands up. "I'm unarmed like you asked."

"Where's your friend, McClain? I told you to bring Mason with you."

"He's close by, keeping an eye on you and me. If there is any gunfire, he's going to alert the police."

"That's not our deal, McClain. I want both of you, not just you."

"No, I'm afraid I'm all you're going to get. Now, where's my wife? I want to see her."

"She's safe inside, but you're not going to see her until I see your friend."

"No, that's not going to happen. I'm all you get, a fair exchange for my wife. You can have me just send out my wife."

"My brother is dead because of you, McClain."

"I don't even know who you are, but I'll take credit for it. I assume you're talking about one of the twins, which would make you a Squires, right?"

"Not exactly. Kyle was my brother, though. And I had to kill him because of you and that detective from Wichita."

"Okay," Booger said. He wanted to keep this guy talking. "Why did you kill Kyle? What did he ever do to you?"

"He brought attention to my little business. He became a liability," Jarvis said with a hint of emotion.

Jarvis' mind flashed to two days earlier. He and

Kyle got into a heated argument.

"This bitch showed up at my house today, Kyle. She was strung out – a real mess. Seems she dated Ben and knew all about your operation. She threatened me. Said she had money. Said she knew people in high places. She stood there in front of my house and told me that that she got my name and address from you and that if I didn't give her a bag of bump, she'd turn me in."

"She's crazy, Jarvis. I didn't tell her anything!"

"This is on you! You brought him in, and he couldn't be trusted!"

"Is that why you killed Kyle? That sort of makes us even, don't you think?" Booger said. "Now, with both brothers out of the way, you're free to run your business however you want."

"Oh, but there's a problem, Mr. McClain. I'm not free just yet. Why don't you come inside so we can talk some more."

"Not before I see my wife."

"McClain, you have five guns pointed directly at your heart. Not coming into my home when I've welcomed you is just rude. And you won't like how I deal with rude men."

"Promise me that you'll let my wife go, and I'll come inside."

"You have my word that I'll let her go."

"Okay, fine then."

Booger walked slowly to the entrance of the house with his hands still up. Including Jarvis, there were five men on the porch waiting for Booger to walk up the steps and enter the house before them. Booger took one, then two steps up the porch stairs before he quickly reached behind his back and pulled out his revolver. He began shooting at the men around him. They returned fire, and a hail of bullets began to fly. Booger was hit almost instantly and fell back off the front of the porch. He was shot in the leg and the arm.

At that very moment, Mason broke through the basement door and began firing. He caught the men off-guard, and the shots penetrated them one after another as they began falling to the ground. In the hail of gunfire, Mason managed to take out everyone except Jarvis, who had jumped off the porch before shooting wildly in Mason's direction.

When the smoke cleared, Jarvis had jumped in his car and sped away. Mason found Booger laying in front of the porch, unable to stand up.

"I've been hit," Booger said. "I'm okay, but I can't move too well. Can you search for the key?"

"Sure, buddy," Mason responded.

One by one, Mason went through the pockets of each of the deceased men. It was in the pockets of the fourth guy he searched that he found a set of keys.

"I'm going to call the police, and then I'll go down to the cage and open it," Mason said.

After calling in the shooting, Mason headed down to the basement. He turned on the lights. That's when he got a good look at the basement. It was more like a cellar than a basement. The walls consisted of bricks. The floor was concrete, with plenty of cracks and uneven parts.

A door at one end of the basement was locked. A table against one wall contained various tools. Mason made his way to the tunnel at the other end of the basement. He crawled through it to the cage.

"Everything's alright," he said to whoever or whatever was inside. "I'm here to get you out."

He tried numerous keys before he found one that would fit the lock. He turned the key and opened the latch. Then opened the cage. Rose was inside, curled up in a fetal position in about three inches of rainwater.

"I'm going to get you out of here, Rose," he said.

"Where's Booger?" Rose asked in a voice that was barely recognizable.

"He's okay. Just took a couple of bullets, but nothing serious. He's waiting upstairs for you."

Once outside the tunnel, Mason carried Rose up the stairs and right to Booger.

"Damn, Rose, you look wonderful," Booger said.

"Well, probably better than you," she said. "Haven't you learned to duck when the bullets start flying?"

"I tried to, but there were bullets all around. And maybe I'm not as fast as I used to be."

"That's an understatement, old man," Rose said as she leaned down to give her husband a gentle kiss on the lips.

Police cars and several ambulances arrived a few minutes later, and both Rose and Booger were taken away to the local hospital. Booger underwent surgery that night for the two bullet wounds. But he was lucky.

Neither bullet penetrated anything vital.

Rose had lost quite a bit of weight, and she suffered from hypothermia. She got a hospital room two doors down from Booger. Both would spend the next several days in the hospital.

They were like newlyweds again, spending all their waking hours together and reminiscing about better times. Eventually, the talk got around to Jarvis.

"Do you think he is the serial killer that struck Wichita?"

"No, but he must have been there. He and Kyle must've been helping Ben towards the end somehow. Jarvis must be the missing half-brother."

"What about the Springfield murders?"

"I believe Wade committed those crimes," Mason said. He was the serial killer both here and in Wichita. His mistake was involving Kyle and Jarvis."

"Ronald Squires was married before," Rose said. "I remember from the records."

"That's right," Booger said.

"Yes, Wade was killing again, but he was also helping make Meth with his brother. All of it brought attention back to Jarvis," Mason said.

"And where is Jarvis now?" Rose asked.

"No one knows," Mason said. "Which means we're not out of danger."

CHAPTER 19
REVENGE

Dressed in black from head to toe, Jarvis parked his car in a vacant lot several blocks away from Booger and Rose's office home. From there, he walked, staying in the shadows as he went. The video surveillance picked up his every movement as he approached, but no one was watching the cameras.

He tried several windows in the front of the building. They were all locked. So, he crept around the back of the building. The lights were off inside, which was understandable. It was nearly 3 in the morning. Hardly anyone was awake at that hour.

Jarvis climbed a fence that surrounded the rear of the house. From the backyard, he was able to gain access to the patio door. A thin metal tool was used to unlock the door. Inside was a bedroom. It was dark and hard to see, but no one was in the bed, and the room appeared empty. The bedroom door was shut. He took out a flashlight, turned it on, and began searching every inch of the room. There was no one there.

Slowly and quietly, he opened the door. Sounds were coming from behind another door. He stopped to listen for a few seconds. "A television set," he said to himself. "Someone must be in that room."

But he wasn't ready to go that way, so he turned in the opposite direction in the hallway. He first went into the bathroom and checked it out. Then he went into the living room, using his flashlight to search every inch of it and the kitchen which adjoined it. He didn't find what he was looking for. So, he headed toward the room with the television on.

When he got to the door, he pulled a gun out of his jacket. He held it with his right hand as he slowly opened the door with his left. Carefully and quietly, he entered the room. That's when he saw the man lying on the couch, sound asleep, with the television on just in front of him. It was Mason. He'd fallen asleep watching the cameras.

Slowly, like a hunter, Jarvis walked toward the man, pointing the gun in his direction in case he woke up or made any sudden movement.

Two feet from the man, he pointed the gun with a silencer attached directly at the man's head.

"You should have let sleeping dogs lie," he said just before he fired two shots. Mason fell and did not move. Blood splattered on Jarvis as he looked down at the man.

Mason, hearing the words, was semi-conscious when the shots that claimed his life rang out. The look on his face was a question. Mason never had time to process what happened. His life ended in that state between awake and asleep.

Jarvis took a towel from the bar on the side of the room and wiped the blood off his face. Then he went back to the man and rummaged through his pockets. After a moment, he found what he was looking for, the keys to the office and his car.

Then he took one final look at the body and smiled. "Now, I can say I've killed a cop."

Mason's death wasn't satisfying, though. It was too easy. And there was more work to be done.

———

Rose and Booger held hands as they walked out the front door of the Mercy-Springfield campus. Nearly dying had given both a new perspective on life. Now they knew what was most important: family. Family for them was each other. Neither had living relatives.

It was a bright, sunny day.

"It's a little chilly. Do you want me to put the top up?" Booger asked.

"No, let's leave it down. It's such a nice day," Rose said.

Mason had driven Booger's cherry red Corvette to the hospital so they could come home in it, but he had forgotten to put the top up.

"Thank goodness it didn't rain," Rose commented. "Speaking of Mason, I thought he would be here today when we got released."

"Oh, he probably got busy. I'm sure he's waiting for us at home."

Booger had become good friends with Mason during the time they spent together. It felt good to have a friend that he knew would protect his back if he needed and he was certain that the detective felt the same way about him.

On the way home, the couple stopped for ice cream. But soon after they pulled into the lot at their office and parked in their usual parking space. Mason's car was there.

Booger pulled out his key and opened the front door to the office building.

"Funny, the inside's dark. Mason must not have turned the lights on."

"Odd," Rose commented.

Booger flipped on the light switches to the lobby and looked around.

"Mason, we're home," he yelled.

There was no response.

"Maybe he's in the house or upstairs in the office," Rose said.

"Yeah, you're probably right."

"I'm going to go upstairs. Do you want to go to rest?"

"Yeah, sounds good, hun."

Rose gave her husband a gentle kiss and then turned left down the hallway to their house. Booger headed up the stairs to his office on the third floor.

When Booger married Rose, he built their house onto the rear of his office building. Everything was under one structure, but the living area and the office section were separate. It was practical and convenient.

Rose unlocked the door to a dark house. She flipped on some lights and yelled, "Mason, are you here?"

There was no answer.

When Booger opened the office door it was dark also. He flipped on the lights and looked around. Mason was not there either. The office looked undisturbed. That was when a chill ran down Booger's back. Mason was nowhere to be found, yet his car was parked in the lot outside.

"Something is wrong," he said to himself.

That's when he picked up the phone and called the house.

Rose answered. "What's up, Booger?"

"Is Mason in the house?"

"No, I don't see him, but the man-cave door is shut, and I hear the television playing in the background. Maybe he's in there. I'm going to check."

"No!" Booger screamed into the phone. "Get out of the house now."

But it was too late. Rose opened the door and saw Mason's body. She let out a blood-curdling scream that caused Booger to drop the phone and run towards her.

Rose's body froze in place. She was unable to move. That was when she saw Jarvis coming toward her. She tried to run. She couldn't.

He had a knife in his hand and a darkness in his eyes like nothing Rose had ever seen before.

He grabbed her with one hand and held the knife against her throat with the other. Then he dragged her to the front door, where he locked and chained the door.

Booger ran frantically down the stairs and down the hallway to the entrance to his house. He tried to open it, but it wouldn't budge. Finally, he began kicking the door. Then, with one run, he managed to break the lock and the chain, and the door flew open.

"Rose," he screamed as he started toward the man cave.

That's when he felt the hammer hit him over the head. He fell to the ground and lost consciousness.

He had no idea how long he was out on that floor, but when he woke, it was completely dark both inside the house and outside. A note had been placed on his body. He read it:

"We're going to play a game of Cat and Mouse. I'm the cat. You're the mouse. Your wife is hidden somewhere in the building. You have thirty minutes to find her before I kill her. But be careful. I'll give you ten minutes, and then I'm going to start hunting you. Your time starts now."

"How could he possibly know that I woke up and read the note to start the clock on the thirty minutes?" Booger asked himself. "The only explanation is that he is watching the video monitors from the security room on the second floor."

Booger thought about going straight to the security room, but chances were that Jarvis left right after seeing Booger read the note.

He reached down for his gun, but it was gone. There was one locked in the office desk on the third floor if he could reach it in time. But now he needed to look for Rose. The lights were completely out, and it was pitch black in the house which made his search that more difficult. He looked meticulously through the house first, every room and closet, as fast as he could manage. She was not there. He had twenty minutes left.

The breaker was off throughout the office and home. There were no lights on anywhere. He managed to feel his way through the hallway and lobby. His eyes were beginning to adjust to the dark, but it was still hard to see things within inches of his face.

From the lobby, he took the stairs up to the second floor. There, he searched the security room and the safe house. There was no sign of Rose. Time was running out. Ten minutes left.

There was only one more floor to check: the third floor. Rose had to be there, but so did Jarvis. He would be waiting for him. Booger had no choice. He had to find his wife before time ran out. He knew it was likely a trap, but he also knew that if he didn't find her in time, Jarvis would definitely kill her.

So, up the stairs he went. Once on the third floor, he went quietly into his office. The lobby was where Rose had her desk. It was dark and cold inside. There was no sign of Rose. "Where is she?" And then he knew. Booger's office had a bathroom. Rose had to be in it.

Booger quietly walked to his desk. Four minutes left now. He pulled out the desk key from his pocket and fiddled with it in the dark, trying to open the desk drawer. Finally, he was able to insert it and turn. The desk drawer made a squeaking noise as it opened. Inside was his gun, and he knew he'd need it. He lifted it out of the drawer and walked toward the bathroom. The door was shut. He turned the doorknob and opened it. When he took a step inside, he heard the shot and saw Jarvis out of the corner of his eye. As he fell to the ground, he saw Rose curled up on the floor, her legs and hands tied.

Just as he was about to hit the floor, he tossed the gun in Rose's direction. Then he hit the ground, blood pouring from his shoulder. Jarvis stood over him and pointed the gun directly at his head.

"I'm going to have a good time with your wife. Then I'm going to kill her, but you won't be around to see it. Shame," Jarvis said, with an evil grin. "You know, Ben was on to something. This is fun."

Then, he pointed his gun at Booger's head, standing just feet away. "Can never be too careful in these situations. So, say goodbye to your wife."

The sound of the gun going off was loud and shook the pictures on the wall.

Hands tied, Rose had managed to pick up the gun. She hit her target true.

"Think again, asshole!" she yelled.

————————

Sirens blared through the dark streets, getting louder as they got closer.

"Hang in there, old man," Rose said. "The ambulance is on the way."

Blood was pouring out of her husband. She had wrapped a sheet tightly around the wound, but he was still losing blood. Booger was drifting in and out of consciousness.

"If you leave me, Booger McClain, I'll never forgive you," Rose said with tears pouring down her face.

But Booger couldn't talk. He couldn't move. All he could do was tighten his grip on Rose's hand until he passed out and his hand went limp.

Booger underwent surgery later that night. Jarvis' bullet was found lodged in the detective's lungs – three inches from his heart. For four hours, he lay on the operating table. Rose walked the hallways, waiting for news from his surgeon.

As the sun began to come up on the next day, Booger was wheeled into a hospital room with Rose by his side.

It would be eight hours later when he woke up.

"Where am I?" he asked.

"Cox South," Rose said, smiling down at him.

"Why are you smiling, Rose?"

"Because I love you," she replied. "And we're safe now."

-THE END-

Alan Brown grew up in the suburbs of Kansas City and graduated from Shawnee Mission East High School in 1973 and Avila University in 1979. Now, he lives in a suburb of St. Louis, MO, with my wife and three daughters. He also has four sons who are grown and living outside the home. He enjoys writing about experiences he had growing up, examining the fantastical side and the dark side of a person's natural fears. All of his books are based on a reality in his life. He is a fan of Alfred Hitchcock. Like his stories, Alan Brown's will conclude with a twist, something he hopes will take the reader by surprise.

Brian Brown: I am a husband, father of four and a former business and political reporter from Springfield, Missouri, who currently lives and works in the St. Louis area. I've written five books with my father, Alan Brown, and edited a sixth. All our novels involve our fictional detective, Booger McClain, in what we have dubbed our Ozarks' Noir style. I'm also an amateur photographer: @Bbrownspfd on Instagram. More information about our novels is available on our Facebook page (Alan and Brian Brown Write Stuff): https://www.facebook.com/profile.php?id=100064104282706.